Samuel French Acting Edition

Love, Lies & The Doctor's Dilemma

An American Farce by
Michael Parker & Susan Parker

SAMUELFRENCH.COM   SAMUELFRENCH.CO.UK

FOR PRODUCTION ENQUIRIES

UNITED STATES AND CANADA
Info@SamuelFrench.com
1-866-598-8449

UNITED KINGDOM AND EUROPE
Plays@SamuelFrench.co.uk
020-7255-4302

Each title is subject to availability from Samuel French, depending
upon country of performance. Please be aware that *LOVE, LIES &
THE DOCTOR'S DILEMMA* may not be licensed by Samuel French in
your territory. Professional and amateur producers should contact the
nearest Samuel French office or licensing partner to verify availability.

MUSIC USE NOTE

Licensees are solely responsible for obtaining formal written permission from copyright owners to use copyrighted music in the performance of this play and are strongly cautioned to do so. If no such permission is obtained by the licensee, then the licensee must use only original music that the licensee owns and controls. Licensees are solely responsible and liable for all music clearances and shall indemnify the copyright owners of the play(s) and their licensing agent, Samuel French, against any costs, expenses, losses and liabilities arising from the use of music by licensees. Please contact the appropriate music licensing authority in your territory for the rights to any incidental music.

IMPORTANT BILLING AND CREDIT REQUIREMENTS

If you have obtained performance rights to this title, please refer to your licensing agreement for important billing and credit requirements.

LOVE, LIES & THE DOCTOR'S DILEMMA was first produced in the United States by Susan Fletcher Lyons at Ed Fletcher's Early Bird Dinner Theatre, Clearwater, Florida on May 7, 2016. The director was Toby Manion and the designers were Toby Manion, Mark Ogden, and Chris Koberna. The cast was as follows:

JOAN SCHELLER	Tracy Borgatti
SANDY	Peter J. Konowicz
VINNY "THE ENFORCER"	Paul Palmisano
OLIVIA ST. CLAIRE	Barbara Anthony
RACHAEL	Selena Vela
CHRIS	Eddy Ganim

LOVE, LIES & THE DOCTOR'S DILEMMA was first produced in Canada by Sandy Fevens at Th'YARC Playhouse and Arts Centre, Yarmouth, Nova Scotia on May 12, 2016. The director was Judy Snow and the designers were Darren Deveau and Gerry Saunders. The cast was as follows:

JOAN SCHELLER	Nicole LeBlanc
SANDY	Dave Sarginson
VINNY "THE ENFORCER"	Jamie LeBlanc
OLIVIA ST. CLAIRE	Jessica DeMille
RACHAEL	Camille Cramm
CHRIS	Jeremy Watkins

CHARACTERS

JOAN SCHELLER – (45+) A middle-aged widow. She lives with her former gardener, Sandy. She is unconventional and free-spirited. In fact, she and Sandy grow small amounts of marijuana for their personal recreational use in a white-washed green house they call the "potting shed." She doesn't seem to care what others think of her, except her sister-in-law Olivia, who seems to dominate her in some strange way. Neither her son, Chris, nor Olivia are aware of Joan's penchant for marijuana or her relationship with Sandy. As Joan interacts with each of the characters, she is quick-thinking and resourceful. Her seemingly innocent white lies create chaos and confusion throughout the play.

SANDY – (45+) An easy-going, mild-mannered guy who appears to be in love with Joan. He was, in fact, her gardener, and began working for her after her husband died. At the very beginning of the play, Sandy and Joan are kissing on the couch, when Olivia arrives unexpectedly and almost catches them. Joan, afraid of Olivia's disapproval, introduces Sandy as Dr. Gardener her psychiatrist, and explains they were simply having a session. Joan has left him no choice but to go along with her deception. Little does he realize that he will be in great demand as a psychiatrist for the rest of the play.

VINNY "THE ENFORCER" – (40+) The quintessential Italian mobster: he dresses like one, he talks like one, and he carries, in a concealed shoulder holster, a magnum .45, which he does not hesitate to show to everyone. He is looking for Joan's son, Chris, who has accumulated considerable gambling debts and is now on the run from the mob. Although he appears tough, we later learn this is all bluff and bluster as he turns out to be a sensitive pussy-cat. He has a rough "New Jersey" accent.

OLIVIA ST. CLAIRE – (40+) Joan's sister-in-law. A wealthy, aging movie star, she never enters a room but always "makes an entrance." A well-meaning but overbearing woman, she asserts her authority upon everyone, especially Joan, who she sees as weak and incapable of taking care of herself since her husband's death. Joan, embarrassed to let Olivia know that her son is in debt to the mob, creates yet another deception and introduces Vinny as her security guard. Olivia appears to be quite taken with the rough and street-smart Vinny.

RACHAEL – (20+) Joan's new neighbor. She seems to live in her own world, constantly being nosey and taking liberties. She continually refers to disastrous incidents in her life, and we soon see why they happened. With her flighty demeanor and malapropisms, you're left to wonder how she ever survives in life. She is, however, a sweet, thoughtful, and kind woman.

CHRIS – (20+) Joan's son who is on the run from the mob. He is seemingly out of work and living a carefree life. He does not seem to take his situation very seriously. Joan, however, takes it extremely seriously and, fearful for his safety, persuades him to masquerade as her daughter, Christina. Later in the play, we discover that he, in fact, works for the FBI as an undercover agent.

SETTING

Joan's Suburban Home, Anytown USA

ACT I: Mid-afternoon

ACT II: The action is continuous

TIME

The Present

ACT I

(It is the living room of **JOAN**'s suburban home. Upstage center is an archway leading to the front door, which is off left. There is a large potted plant in the entrance way. Downstage left are double French doors, leading to the garden and pool house. Above them on the left wall is a bar, with two stools on the downstage side. Behind the bar on the left wall is a window, which is open and large enough for an actor to get through. On the back wall of the bar are shelves with glasses, perhaps a small wine rack, bar decorations, and the key to the potting shed. Downstage right is an open archway leading to bedrooms and the rest of the house. Upstage right is a double-hinged door to the kitchen, which leads to the back door. Below it is a couch, with decorative cushions and an afghan; to its right an end table; and in front of it a low coffee table. To the left of the couch and slightly downstage is a low back easy chair. On the rear wall behind the couch is a door to a broom closet. The decor is bright and tasteful.)

(The curtain rises on an empty set. After a moment or two, **JOAN** enters from the kitchen. She is dressed in a casual skirt or pants and a colorful blouse. She wears little make-up. Her hair is loose and natural. She is carrying a small tray with a newspaper, two coffee mugs, and a small plate of brownies. She comes down and places the tray on the coffee table, then crosses left to the French doors.)

JOAN. *(Calling.)* Sandy, Sandy, coffee's ready. *(She heads back and sits on the couch right end.)*

SANDY. *(Enters from the French doors, leaving them open, and crosses toward* **JOAN**. *He is wearing khaki pants, a button-down collared shirt, and loafers. He is carrying a single rose.)* Good morning Joan. You're looking beautiful today.

JOAN. Thank you. You were up bright and early this morning.

SANDY. Well, I wanted to do a little gardening, I may not officially be employed as your gardener anymore, but I still take pride in how the garden looks. *(Hands her the rose.)* Here you go my dear, happy birthday.

JOAN. *(Puts the rose on the tray.)* Thank you love. The coffee is hot and the brownies are freshly baked this morning. *(Takes a bite of brownie.)*

SANDY. *(Sits on the left side of couch.)* Ah, our morning brownies, what would we do without them?

JOAN. Have a boring day I'd imagine. By the way, did you check on the marijuana plants in the potting shed while you were out there? I used most of what we had in these brownies. Do we still have any plants left?

SANDY. The plants are fine. I make sure that we have three or four small pots growing at all times. It's enough for us. *(Picks up a brownie and takes a bite.)*

JOAN. I know, I know, we really only need ten milligrams per batch, but I just don't want to run out. It's not like I can pick it up at the supermarket. By the way dear, I forgot to tell you, we have a new neighbor.

SANDY. Oh?

JOAN. She came over yesterday and introduced herself while you were in town.

SANDY. What's she like?

JOAN. Youngish, different. Her name's Rachael.

SANDY. Different? How?

JOAN. For starters, she never used the front door, walked right in through the garden. Scared me half to death.

Floated around here like a butterfly, poking her nose into all the rooms. To top it off, she took one of the brownies and ate it before I could stop her.

SANDY. Besides being different, was she nice?

JOAN. I suppose, though we had the strangest conversation, half the time I didn't have a clue what she was saying.

SANDY. Why is she a foreigner?

JOAN. Yes, she's from [**name a neighboring state or small town**].

SANDY. *(Laughing.)* She sounds interesting, I'll look forward to meeting her sometime. *(Stands, hands* JOAN *the newspaper, and picks up the tray.)* My turn for kitchen duty, you just relax and read the paper. *(Exits to the kitchen.)*

> (JOAN *opens the paper and starts to read as* VINNY *appears in the French doors, which are open. He is dressed like a typical mobster. He wears a dark, double-breasted suit, white socks, yellow shirt, red tie, and a black fedora. Under the jacket he has a shoulder holster, with a huge magnum .45 automatic.)*

VINNY. *(Steps into the room.)* Hey, you there, lady.

JOAN. *(Puts down the paper and stands.)* Who are you? What are you doing here?

VINNY. The name's Vinny.

JOAN. Vinny who?

VINNY. Vinny the Enforcer. I'm looking for Mrs. Scheller. I'd like to have a little chat with her.

JOAN. That would be me. What do you want?

VINNY. Good, sit down.

JOAN. *(Ignores him and continues to stand.)* Now look here, you can't just come barging into my house telling me what to do.

VINNY. *(Opens his jacket and shows her the gun.)* Listen little lady, when ya got "Big Bertha" here, you can do what ya want.

JOAN. You call your gun Bertha?

VINNY. Yeah, ain't she a beauty?

JOAN. Bertha or not, you need to remove yourself from my house.

VINNY. Or else what?

JOAN. I'll call the police.

VINNY. *(Wanders right.)* Now, that would be a bad idea, a very bad idea.

JOAN. And would you care to tell me why?

VINNY. When I came through the garden, I couldn't help but notice that little green house with the white-washed glass, and that big lock on the door.

JOAN. Oh, you mean our potting shed.

VINNY. Potting shed! Good one Mrs. Scheller, but ya know what I smelled lady? Weed, pot, grass, cannabis, call it what ya want, marijuana.

JOAN. You're wrong.

VINNY. Listen lady, when ya been on the streets your whole life, and you're in my line of work, ya know weed when ya smell it.

JOAN. Oh dear. *(Sits on the couch.)* It's only such a very little bit.

VINNY. We both know it ain't legal. So you still want to call the cops?

JOAN. I guess not.

VINNY. So, Mrs. Scheller, *(Starts to pace down left.)* ya gonna cooperate?

JOAN. By the way, how do you know my name?

VINNY. It's my business to know. I'm looking for your kid, Christopher.

JOAN. Why?

VINNY. Let's just say he's been a bad boy.

JOAN. It's not a woman again is it?

VINNY. It's not fast women, it's slow horses. He's been gambling on the ponies, and I represent the bookies. They want their dough.

JOAN. *(Stands.)* Well Mr. Enforcer, you've come to the wrong place. He doesn't live here and I haven't seen him or spoken to him in months. So I think it's best that you leave now.

VINNY. We got reason to believe your son's gonna come running to Mama for the money, so Mrs. Scheller, I'll just be stick'n around and drop'n in from time to time. The boys don't like it when they don't get paid.

JOAN. I think you're wasting your time, but the next time you do, would you kindly use the front door.

VINNY. In my line of work, we don't usually use front doors. *Ciao. (Exits through the French doors, but quickly sticks his head back in.)* Oh yeah, some friendly advice. Plant some strong scented something outside the greenhouse. Maybe some Jasmines, they have a real nice smell. *(Exits, leaving the doors open.)*

JOAN. Oh dear. *(Quickly moves to the kitchen door and calls offstage.)* Sandy, Sandy, come quick! *(Runs left to the French doors and looks into the garden.)*

SANDY. *(Enters from the kitchen and moves toward* JOAN.*)* Joan, are you alright? You sound upset.

JOAN. *(Quickly moves right, and they hug.)* You aren't going to believe what just happened. We're in trouble.

SANDY. Okay sweetie, come and sit down. Now tell me what's got you in such a state. (JOAN *sits on the couch right and* SANDY *sits on the couch center. They hold hands.)*

JOAN. It's Chris.

SANDY. Now what's he done?

JOAN. He appears to be in trouble with the mob. He's run up gambling debts and they've sent this guy called Vinny the Enforcer to take care of it. They think he's going to come here, so this Vinny guy is going to be hanging around waiting for him.

SANDY. Okay, that's not the end of the world. Chris hasn't been here in years, in fact, I've never met him. Even though it's your birthday, I doubt he'll show up.

JOAN. I agree, but that's not all. This guy, the Enforcer, knows about the potting shed.

SANDY. What?

JOAN. He says he could smell the pot.

SANDY. Who is this guy? He must have a nose like a bloodhound. What's he going to do?

JOAN. Actually, come to think of it, I don't think he's going to do anything, except hang around and wait for Chris to show up. *(Stands up.)* Oh my gosh. Oh no! Have you forgotten who's coming today? *(Rushes to the closet and gets the vacuum cleaner.)*

SANDY. Olivia? That's right, she's here for your birthday. What are you doing?

JOAN. What does it look like I'm doing. *(Leaving the vacuum cleaner just behind the chair, she moves behind the bar with the cord.)* Olivia's arriving and the house is a disaster. *(Bends down as if plugging it in, but doesn't get the chance.)*

SANDY. Looks fine to me.

JOAN. *(Pops up.)* Of course it does, that's because you're a man and not a woman. *(Moves right to the vacuum and frantically works the on/off switch, which doesn't go on.)* It's not working.

SANDY. No kidding.

JOAN. Well, don't just sit there, do something.

SANDY. What do you want me to do? I don't know anything about vacuum cleaners.

JOAN. Well, couldn't you at least look at it? *(SANDY leans slightly to his left and stares intently at the vacuum cleaner.)* You know I didn't mean that. Do something, please, she'll be here any minute now. *(SANDY stands and kicks the vacuum cleaner, then tries the switch. It still doesn't work.)* Wait, I know, go get the manual. It's in that cardboard box in the closet. *(JOAN continues to fiddle with the vacuum.)*

SANDY. *(Moves to the closet door and enters, then turns.)* Are you sure it's plugged in? *(Disappears back into the closet.)*

(JOAN looks at the closet and then moves left behind the bar and bends down as if plugging it in. She moves right to the vacuum cleaner and tries the switch. This time it works.)

(Steps out of the closet.) What happened?

JOAN. It suddenly started working.

SANDY. Really? Just like that? *(Snaps his fingers.)*

JOAN. Yes.

SANDY. *(Comes up behind her and wraps his arms around her.)* You know, for someone who's only recently taken up lying, you're showing a real flair for it. *(He kisses the top of her head.)*

JOAN. *(Steps away and turns toward him.)* Oh Sandy, I really wish Olivia wasn't coming today. I'm just not ready for her to be here.

SANDY. *(Takes the vacuum cleaner and leaves it in front of the right end of the bar back. He then crosses back to JOAN and takes her hand, leading her to the couch.)* I don't know why you're so worried, the house looks perfectly alright, but you look like a wreck. Come sit down and tell me what's got you so upset. *(SANDY sits left and JOAN sits center.)*

JOAN. You know, I tried to tell her she didn't have to come, but Olivia only listens to Olivia. Sandy, my love, I have to confess something to you. I know you've never met her, but Olivia is obnoxious, overbearing, pretentious, self-righteous, filthy rich, and a thousand other words I could use to describe her, but she is my late husband's sister.

SANDY. Oh come on, she can't be all that bad.

JOAN. You don't think so? Her idea of a bad neighborhood is if the local deli doesn't have valet parking. To be honest, she is the only person who makes me feel… well, inferior, and I don't want her to know that we live together. She will moralize till the cows come home, and it's just not worth it. She'll be saying, "Poor Joan, Poor Joan," all day. So please, just for today, can I tell her you're my gardener and not the love of my life?

SANDY. Poor Joan.

JOAN. Don't you start, I'm just not ready to answer questions about us yet, at least not to her.

SANDY. Poor Joan. (**JOAN** *hits him with a pillow.*) Alright, love, what ever makes you happy. (**JOAN** *puts her arms around* **SANDY**'s *neck and kisses him.* **SANDY** *leans into her and she scoots further down, with her legs up on the couch as they continue to kiss.*)

OLIVIA. (*Enters from the front door. She is wearing a tailored skirt and designer blouse. She has a matching hat, handbag, and shoes, and is wearing large sunglasses. Her hair is elegantly coiffured, her make-up is perfect, perhaps even a little overdone, and her nails are neatly manicured. She looks every bit the movie star she once was. She is carrying a gift basket with two bottles of wine and balloons.*) Hellooooo... (*At this point* **JOAN** *is lying on the couch, head right and feet left, with* **SANDY** *almost on top of her. In the two seconds it takes* **OLIVIA** *to round the corner from the front door and come downstage,* **SANDY** *leaps to his feet and is standing at the left end of the couch, leaving* **JOAN** *still lying down.*) Joan, what are you doing on the couch? It's the middle of the day. Who is this man?

JOAN. (*Quickly stands up.*) Er, er...ah, the couch, yes...this man...yes.

OLIVIA. (*More demanding.*) Yes, what are you doing on the couch, and who is this man?

JOAN. (*Looks at* **SANDY.**) He's...er...er...he's my... psychiatrist!

SANDY. What?

JOAN. We were having a session.

SANDY. What?

OLIVIA. (*Deflated.*) Oh, I didn't know you were in therapy. Poor Joan. I just knew it would come to this. (*Hands* **JOAN** *the balloons and wine.*) Here, these are for you dear, Happy Birthday.

JOAN. (*Puts them on the bar back right side.*) Thank you, that was very kind of you.

OLIVIA. Nonsense. Now, are you going to introduce us?

JOAN. *(Comes down.)* Yes, of course, this is…er, er…Doctor Gardener.

SANDY. What?

JOAN. Doctor Gardener, this is my sister-in-law, Olivia St. Claire.

SANDY. *(Shakes hands.)* Hello Ms. St. Claire, it's a real pleasure to meet you.

OLIVIA. Of course it is. Please, call me Olivia. A psychiatrist who makes house calls, that's very unusual.

JOAN. Well, Doctor Gardener is a very unusual doctor. He likes to get out of his office. Sometimes he stays all afternoon just relaxing in the garden. Don't you Doctor Gardener?

SANDY. Er… I guess I do. *(Looks at* **JOAN.***)* May I have a word with you?

JOAN. Sure. *(She and* **SANDY** *move downstage left a few steps, followed by* **OLIVIA.***)*

SANDY. I meant we should be alone.

OLIVIA. *(Looks around.)* We are alone.

JOAN. What Doctor Gardner meant was…

OLIVIA. Well, as you appear to have nothing to contribute to this conversation, why don't you take this time to go and relax in the garden. I would like to have a private word with Joan.

SANDY. So would I! (**JOAN** *gives him a look.)* Right, I'll be in the garden.

OLIVIA. Good then, off you go. *(She ushers him out the French doors, turns, and goes to the bar.)* Well Joan, while I pour myself a drink, why don't you tell me why you need a psychiatrist. *(Goes behind the bar and pours herself a drink.)* You know you can always talk to me.

JOAN. *(Perches on the left arm of the couch, facing left.)* Actually, I…

OLIVIA. Poor Joan. I know how difficult it has been for you since my brother died. How are you coping?

JOAN. As a matter of fact I…

OLIVIA. Obviously not well, I mean if you need a psychiatrist and all. Is he any good?

JOAN. It's difficult to say, I…

OLIVIA. Well, I must say he is very attractive. You know, while I'm here, I think I'll arrange to have a session with him.

JOAN. I don't think…

OLIVIA. Poor Joan. It's quite obvious, that I've been neglecting you, so I decided that I would come stay with you for the next few weeks and keep you company. (JOAN *springs to her feet with a look of abject horror on her face.*) You, living here, all alone. Poor Joan. We'll have a grand time. Of course I will have to work on my autobiography while I'm here, but I'll make sure I leave time to spend with you.

JOAN. That's very kind of you but…

OLIVIA. Good, that's all settled then. Now which room will I be in?

VINNY. (*Enters from the front door and moves downstage.*) Ciao again. Ya know, Mrs. Scheller, you really should lock your doors, you never know who might show up.

OLIVIA. Joan, why is this strange man in your house?

VINNY. (*To* OLIVIA.) Who ya calling strange? (*To* JOAN.) Who's this?

OLIVIA. I'm Joan's sister-in-law, Olivia St. Claire, (*Moves right from behind the bar.*) and who are you?

JOAN. This is Vinny.

OLIVIA. Does he have a last name?

VINNY. I do, but I'm usually called Vinny the…

JOAN. Security guard. Vinny is my security guard, aren't you Vinny.

VINNY. Well, er…er…

OLIVIA. Joan, why do you need a security guard?

JOAN. Vinny, why do I need a security guard?

VINNY. Jeez, Mrs. Scheller, you know why, I gotta catch me a slimeball.

JOAN. What he means is, he is here to make sure the house is safe, isn't that right Vinny.

VINNY. Yeah, I gotta catch me a certain slimeball.

OLIVIA. There are slimeballs in your neighborhood? Poor Joan.

JOAN. Well as you can see there are none of those er... slime things here right now.

OLIVIA. Quite right, but my car is parked on the street. Come along Vinny, you can make yourself useful and escort me to my car. I need to move it and bring in my suitcase. *(She exits the front door as* **VINNY** *stands still in a state of shock.* **OLIVIA** *quickly re-enters.)* NOW VINCENT. *(She turns with a flourish and exits, followed by* **VINNY**.*)*

SANDY. *(Enters from the French doors.)* Joan, who was that guy?

JOAN. That was Vinny, the Enforcer. But Olivia thinks he's my security guard.

SANDY. Why does she think that Joan?

JOAN. Well, er...well, I kind of said he was. I can't let Olivia know he's a mobster looking for Chris.

SANDY. Wonderful. You now have a lover who's a gardener, a gardener who's a psychiatrist, and a mobster who's a security guard.

JOAN. Well I had to do something.

SANDY. Joan, this is getting out of hand. I think it would be better if you just came clean and told the truth.

JOAN. I can't.

SANDY. Why not?

JOAN. Olivia wants to have a session with you while she's here.

SANDY. Are you out of your mind! That's impossible! I can't have a session with her. I think in your delusional state you've forgotten... I'm not a real psychiatrist. I wouldn't have a clue as to what to say or do.

JOAN. Oh, that's easy... You just ask, "What's your problem?" and when she asks a question, you say, "What do you think?"

SANDY. I think you've had one too many brownies. YOU need a psychiatrist...a real one!

OLIVIA. *(Enters through the front door carrying two wigs on stands [see Authors' Notes], followed by* VINNY, *who is carrying a large suitcase.)* Come along Vincent, no dilly-dallying.

VINNY. Jeez, how many times I gotta tell ya, it's Vinny.

OLIVIA. Nonsense, Vincent is much more sophisticated and it's "How many times must I tell you."

VINNY. *(Drops the suitcase in front of* JOAN.*)* Boy, she may be a looker, but that is one tough sister-in-law ya got there. *(Looks at* SANDY.*)* Who's this?

JOAN. Doctor Gardener, may I introduce you to Vinny.

OLIVIA. Joan's security guard.

VINNY. Doctor Gardener?

OLIVIA. Joan's psychiatrist.

VINNY. You one of them shrink guys? Sorry Mrs. Scheller, didn't know you were a wacko.

OLIVIA. Poor Joan.

SANDY. Well I wouldn't exactly describe her as a wacko, *(Looks at* JOAN.*)* however, I can tell you she does have a tendency to exaggerate and stray from the truth.

JOAN. Well, isn't truth in the eye of the beholder?

SANDY. Then you should make an eye doctor appointment...soon.

OLIVIA. Instability and bad eyes? Poor Joan. It's a good thing I'm here. Now, come along, I want to look at the rooms and see which one would be appropriate for me. *(Exits down right, followed by* JOAN *carrying the suitcase.)*

VINNY. Listen Doc, this must be one of them serendipity things, cause lately I've been thinkin' I need to talk to someone, but in my line of work ya just don't do that. But I'm see'n an opportunity here, and you seem like a regular kind of Joe. *(Moves right toward the couch.)* I'll pay the freight whatever it is. *(Sits in the middle of the couch.)*

SANDY. Vinny, I really can't do that.

VINNY. Jeez Doc, come and sit down. *(Pulls out a wad of bills.)* How much is it gonna cost me?

SANDY. *(Sits in the chair.)* Really Vinny, this isn't a good idea.

VINNY. Hows about five big ones. *(Lays them on the coffee table and lies down on the couch, head right, feet left.)* You know Doc, I've never done this before and I'm kinda nervous.

SANDY. Me too.

VINNY. *(Sits up.)* What?

SANDY. What I mean is, I'm not really a psychiatrist.

VINNY. And I'm not really a security guard, I'm an Enforcer. Now that I've told ya, I know ya can't divulge this to anyone, 'cause of that hippopotamus oath you guys take. *(Lies back down.)* Ya know Doc, you're a real smart guy, making me feel comfortable by telling me you're not a shrink. Boy, that's good.

SANDY. *(There is an awkward pause.)* Er... Er... So, what's your problem?

VINNY. The thing is Doc I don't really like my work anymore, I can whack 'em, grill 'em, and I'm really good at thumbscrews, but deep down, I just don't like it no more. Guess I'm just a big ol' softy. Do ya think I need more in life?

SANDY. Er...er... What do you think?

VINNY. Guess, I'm feelin' kinda lonely. I'm just not gettin' any lovin' in my life. What should I do Doc?

SANDY. *(Pauses.)* Er... What do you think?

VINNY. I don't think I got nothin' in my life that means anything to me, except for Bertha.

SANDY. Tell me about Bertha.

VINNY. Well, first off, she's one big mother. She's been with me for lots of years, and we've seen a lot of action together. But she's just not enough for me no more I've been thinking I need to settle down, get me a wife. Do ya think that's a good idea?

SANDY. What do you think?

VINNY. Well, as long as I can keep Bertha

SANDY. You want a wife and Bertha?

VINNY. Yeah, why not?

SANDY. Well, wives don't usually understand about things like Bertha.

VINNY. Jeez Doc. I can't give her up. I don't get no respect without her. What should I do?

SANDY. Er...er... What do you think?

VINNY. Oh, you're good Doc. You're really good. Ya know, I saw this shrink on the telly once, and he always answered a question with a question.

SANDY. Listen Vinny, just for the record, I think that if you're going to get a wife, you must get rid of Bertha.

VINNY. You could be right Doc. But, maybe I could keep Bertha hidd'n away. Maybe in time the little wifey would understand.

SANDY. You haven't had a lot of experience with women have you Vinny?

VINNY. I guess not.

SANDY. Oh dear. How did I get into this mess.

VINNY. I mean I can't just discard Bertha, like she's meant nothin' to me. She needs to be taken care of. She's given me years of good service, and deserves better.

SANDY. Years of good service?

VINNY. Yes. What do I do with her Doc?

SANDY. Oh dear. I think...er... *(Looks at his watch.)* That's it, times up, time for you to go. *(SANDY picks up the money and hands it to* VINNY.*)* This one's on the house.

VINNY. *(Stands and puts the money in his pocket.)* Jeez, I really owe you one Doc. Well, if ya ever need to have somebody roughed up or somethin', I'm your man.

SANDY. *(Tries ushering him to the front door. Noises off,* **JOAN** *and* **OLIVIA** *from the bedrooms.)* I don't think that will be necessary.

VINNY. In my line of work we don't forget favors. *(Cracks his knuckles.)* You're no schmuck Doc, putting me at ease by telling me you're not a psychiatrist, then helping me decide to keep Bertha and get a wife. Mrs. Scheller's a lucky lady to have you for a shrink. *Ciao. (Exits through the front door.)*

SANDY. Oh dear, did I say that?

OLIVIA. *(Enters from down right, followed by* **JOAN**.*)* I will definitely need a lighted make-up mirror, and a few other things, but overall it will have to do. Oh, hello Doctor Gardener, has Vincent left already?

SANDY. Yes, but I have a feeling he'll be back.

> *(Enter* **RACHAEL** *from the French doors. She is dressed casually in a dress with a camisole slip underneath and tennis shoes. Her make-up looks natural and her hairstyle is casual. She is carrying an empty plate.)*

RACHAEL. Helloooo! Oh Joan, I'm so sorry, I didn't know you had company.

JOAN. That's alright, this is my sister-in-law, Olivia St. Claire and er – er – Doctor Gardener. This is Rachael, my new next-door neighbor.

RACHAEL. *(Waves the plate at them.)* Hi. Wow, you're a doctor? You must have an inedible brain *[see Authors' Note]*.

SANDY. Let's hope so.

OLIVIA. Doctor Gardener is a psychiatrist.

RACHAEL. Really? I once had a psychiatric evacuation.

SANDY. Let's hope not!

RACHAEL. *(Almost ignoring everyone, she wanders around, looks behind the bar, opens the closet door and looks in, then has a quick look in the kitchen.)* When I was quite young, I thought I wanted a career in law enforcement, and guess what? I got into the police academy. It didn't work out though because there was a teensy misunderstanding about a paper we had to write.

JOAN. Oh dear.

RACHAEL. It really wasn't my fault. The paper was on grilling tactics, but I accidentally wrote down techniques. I thought it was a little strange, but I wrote in great detail about how it was always best to go slow, and then gradually turn up the heat until the skin is seared, but not burned and to continue for as long as necessary.

SANDY. Oh dear.

RACHAEL. I thought it was a well-written paper, but when I got it back, they said they found my methods too extreme, and the fact that I enjoyed it was simply not acceptable. Before I could explain, they dropped me from the program and sent me for a psychiatric evacuation. Go figure.

OLIVIA. Astonishing.

RACHAEL. *(Stops in front of* **JOAN.***)* Joan, I was wondering if you could spare a few brownies. I can't seem to stop thinking about them. I've never tasted anything quite so good.

JOAN. I'm afraid they're all gone.

RACHAEL. Oh, that's too bad. Maybe you could give me the recipe?

SANDY. I'm sorry, it's a secret family recipe.

RACHAEL. *(Turns to* **OLIVIA.***)* Wait a minute, wait a minute, did you say Olivia St. Claire?

JOAN. Yes I did.

RACHAEL. As in Olivia St. Claire the movie star?

JOAN. I'm afraid so.

RACHAEL. Oh my! *(She rushes over to* **OLIVIA.***)* I didn't recognize you. I was a huge fan of yours. When I was a teenager I saw every single one of your movies.

OLIVIA. Thank you, I think! It really wasn't that long ago.

RACHAEL. I know, I know. Oh-oh-oh. I'm an actress too.

OLIVIA. Really?

RACHAEL. Yes. In high school I was in the end of the year play and got a standing ovulation.

SANDY. Really?

RACHAEL. Yes, it was my first one ever.

OLIVIA. The mind boggles!

RACHAEL. I don't suppose – No. I couldn't ask.

JOAN. I'll bet you're going to!

RACHAEL. Well, I've got an audition for the community theatre tomorrow. Would you read a segment or two with me and give me some pointers.

OLIVIA. Well I don't usually –

RACHAEL. *(Grabs* OLIVIA*'s hand and starts shaking her arm.)* Please, please.

OLIVIA. *(Breaking free of* RACHAEL*'s grip.)* Okay, I suppose I could make an exception.

RACHAEL. Thank you, thank you, oh, I'm going to be working with the great Olivia St. Claire. This is so much better than when I was crowned Miss Dairy Queen of **[insert the name of a local small town]**. You know, that would have been a great evening if it wasn't for the cows that escaped and started a stampede. But it really wasn't my fault. I was just strolling the fair grounds when I tripped and fell into someone who fell into a gate that apparently wasn't latched tight. They blamed me and I was forced to give up my title, even though they did eventually round up all the cows. Anyways, this is so much more exciting. I'll be right back with the script. *(Runs out the French doors.)*

OLIVIA. My, she's an interesting character. I just hope I survive the reading. *(Moves to the bar to get a drink.)* Now, Doctor Gardener, I'd like to discuss setting up a time for a session with you.

SANDY. I'm not sure that would be a good idea.

OLIVIA. Nonsense, you're a therapist and I need therapy.

JOAN. You're right about that.

OLIVIA. What did you say?

JOAN. I said, I doubt that.

OLIVIA. Poor Joan. *(To* SANDY.*)* You don't appear overly busy at the moment, so perhaps now would be an excellent time for a session. *(Moves right toward the couch and sits.)* Please, excuse us Joan. Sit down Doctor Gardener. *(She lies down, head left.)*

JOAN. *(Gently pushes* SANDY *toward the chair.)* I'm sure Olivia's session will be much more interesting than mine. Now, if you'll excuse me, I'll just be in the kitchen. I think I'll make a fresh batch of brownies. I have a feeling we're going to need them. *(Exits to the kitchen.)*

SANDY. *(Sits in the chair.)* Ms. St. Claire, don't you have your own therapist back home?

OLIVIA. Please, call me Olivia. Of course I do, I am a movie star after all.

SANDY. Wouldn't you feel more comfortable talking with him or her?

OLIVIA. They're not here, you are, and I need to talk.

(Looks over at SANDY.*)*

Aren't you going to take notes?

SANDY. Do you want me to?

OLIVIA. All my other therapists have.

SANDY. Right. Let me get a pad and pencil. *(Stands, moves behind the bar, and bends down out of sight.)*

OLIVIA. *(Not heard by* SANDY.*)* What I want to discuss is my sex life.

SANDY. *(Pokes his head up.)* Hold on a sec, can't find a pencil. *(Ducks down behind the bar again.)*

OLIVIA. Yes, I definitely need some help with my sex life these days. I need to spice up my autobiography.

SANDY. *(Moves downstage toward the chair with a pad of paper and a pencil.)* Okay, I'm ready to take notes. *(Sits in the chair.)* So, what's your problem?

OLIVIA. Well, I'm not as active as I used to be.

SANDY. Now that is something I can help you with.

OLIVIA. You can?

SANDY. Of course. Have you thought about joining a club?

OLIVIA. There are clubs?

SANDY. Certainly, I belong to one myself.

OLIVIA. You do?

SANDY. To start you'll want to hire a personal instructor to get back into the swing of things.

OLIVIA. A personal instructor?

SANDY. It was the best thing I ever did.

OLIVIA. Really?

SANDY. Oh, yes, they're very knowledgeable and they give you a lot of hands-on help.

OLIVIA. Hands-on help?

SANDY. Well, some of the equipment is a little tricky at first.

OLIVIA. Equipment?

SANDY. Once you get going, they even have group classes.

OLIVIA. Group classes?

SANDY. They've got beginners all the way up to advanced.

OLIVIA. Advanced?

SANDY. I don't like to brag, but I am part of the advanced group. I'm sure it wouldn't take you long before you were joining us.

OLIVIA. Join you? I don't think I could do that.

SANDY. Of course you could. It's much more fun in a group. As a matter of fact, I'd be happy to introduce you if you'd like to come and meet them all.

OLIVIA. Meet them? *(Sits up.)* I really don't think I would go for this group thing. I must say Dr. Gardener, you are a most unusual psychiatrist.

SANDY. You don't know the half of it.

OLIVIA. I don't think I want to know the half of it.

> *(Enter* **RACHAEL** *through the French doors, carrying a script.)*

RACHAEL. Oh, am I interrupting something?

OLIVIA. Not at all. Thank you Doctor Gardener, you've given me some things to consider.

SANDY. *(Stands and moves to the bar to return the paper and pencil.)* Right, glad I could help. I can see you're going to be busy, so if you'll excuse me, I'll just pop into the kitchen to see how Joan... I mean Mrs. Scheller is doing. *(Exits to the kitchen.)*

RACHAEL. I can't thank you enough for helping me.

OLIVIA. It's the least I could do. After all you are a fan of mine. *(She crosses right and sits on the couch center.)* Now, what's this play all about?

RACHAEL. *(Sits on OLIVIA's left, almost touching her.)* It's about a drug cartel, and the role I want is that of an undercover agent who has filintrated the cartel headquarters.

OLIVIA. *(Inches right.)* Filintrated?

RACHAEL. *(Inches right.)* Yes, you know they don't know she's an agent.

OLIVIA. *(Inches right.)* Go on. What's my role?

RACHAEL. *(Inches right.)* Well, the scene I'm worried about is when this agent realizes she can't go it alone and needs help, so she approaches a woman whom she thinks might be willing to help her.

OLIVIA. *(Attempts to move but is up against the couch arm.)* And that's me?

RACHAEL. Yes

OLIVIA. Okay, let's get started. *(RACHAEL opens the script and places it on the coffee table. Because they are both reading from the one script, RACHAEL has her back to the French doors, and OLIVIA is turned downstage with her head down, bent over the script.)* I'll begin here. *(Reading.)* Why are you acting so strangely? What's going on?

RACHAEL. *(Reading, in a very awkward manner.)* I just don't want anyone to overhear us. Yesterday I noticed that when one of the bosses talked about killing two of the villagers, you looked horrified.

OLIVIA. *(Reading.)* Well I was. Why can't they stop all this bloodshed and murdering. I'm sick of it. I want out.

RACHAEL. *(Reading.)* That's what I thought. *(Enter* **VINNY** *from the garden. He is about to step into the room, but stops dead in his tracks on* **RACHAEL**'*s next line.)* I have something very important to tell you, but I'll need you to keep my secret. Do you promise?

OLIVIA. Yes.

RACHAEL. I am not who everybody thinks I am. *(***VINNY**, *visible to the audience, but not to* **RACHAEL** *or* **OLIVIA**, *stays just outside the French doors, listening.)*

OLIVIA. *(Reading.)* What do you mean?

RACHAEL. *(Reading.)* I'm an undercover agent working for The DEA, my job is to bust this thing wide open. *(***VINNY** *reacts.)* And I need your help.

OLIVIA. *(Reading.)* My help! What can I do?

RACHAEL. *(Reading.)* I'm going to have to produce some hard evidence. Enough to put them behind bars, which means I need to go places I'm not supposed to. I may need you to cover for me.

OLIVIA. *(Reading.)* I suppose I could do that. *(***VINNY** *reacts, then exits to the garden.* **OLIVIA** *sits back in her seat.)* You know my dear, that was a good start, but I have a couple of pointers for you.

RACHAEL. You do? That would be awesome. Thanks.

OLIVIA. Before announcing you're an agent, perhaps you could pause, look around to make quite sure no one is going to overhear you, then lean in confidentially.

RACHAEL. That's brilliant. I love it. Do you suppose you could just show me?

OLIVIA. Of course. What's your line? *(***RACHAEL** *points to the line.)* Right, well this is what I would do. *(Demonstrates furtively looking around, pauses, then leans forward toward* **RACHAEL**, *indicating with a hand motion for her to lean in.)* "I'm an undercover agent working for the DEA." Now, you try it.

RACHAEL. *(Tries to copy* **OLIVIA**, *but ends up with over-exaggerated movements which should show how inexperienced* *she really is as an actress.)* I'm an undercover agent working for the DOA.

OLIVIA. Dead on arrival?

RACHAEL. What? Oh, *(Looks at the script.)* I mean DEA. So, how did I do?

OLIVIA. A little practice wouldn't hurt.

RACHAEL. That's a great idea. Thank you so much Ms. St. Claire, I can't wait to tell everyone who coached me on my audition segment. *(Gives her an overdone hug.)*

OLIVIA. Maybe we should just keep that our little secret.

RACHAEL. Okay. *(Stands.)* Oh Ms. St. Claire, you've been a great perspiration to me. I can't thank you enough. *(Clearly excited.)* Oh, oh, oh... I can't wait to practice. *(Exits through the French doors, leaving her script on the table.)*

(Enter JOAN and SANDY from the kitchen.)

JOAN. Hi Olivia, how did the audition practice go?

OLIVIA. *(Laughs.)* Well she's certainly enthusiastic.

SANDY. Is that a nice way of saying she needs a new hobby?

OLIVIA. Well, we can't all be me. So Joan, I'm a little hungry, how are the brownies coming?

JOAN. I didn't think you ate chocolate. There are a few left from earlier, but the fresh batch is still in the oven. Are you sure I can't get you something else?

OLIVIA. No, I'll wait for the fresh baked brownies, they sound wonderful.

JOAN. Oh dear.

OLIVIA. Poor Joan, I know baking was never your forte, but I'm sure they'll be fine. I haven't had a brownie in years. Call me when they're ready, I'll be in my room. *(Exits down right.)*

SANDY. Can you see her after eating a brownie? Maybe it would mellow her out.

JOAN. *(Sits on the couch right side.)* Olivia, mellow! If she ate a whole panful that wouldn't happen. Looks like we have a moment alone, come sit down and tell me all about your session with her. I'm dying to find out.

SANDY. *(Sits on the couch left side.)* We can't talk about that?

JOAN. Why not?

SANDY. Well, it would be unethical and unprofessional.

JOAN. You do realize you're not really a psychiatrist. Don't you?

SANDY. Of course I do.

JOAN. So, come on, spill the beans.

SANDY. I wouldn't feel right, she trusts me. I can tell you it wasn't anything exciting.

JOAN. Oh, Sandy, you really are a lovely man.

SANDY. *(Puts his arm around* **JOAN.***)* Thank you. *(Kisses her.)*

(Enter **VINNY** *from the front door.)*

VINNY. Jeez, sorry Doc. Didn't mean to interrupt.

*(**JOAN** and **SANDY** both quickly stand.)*

JOAN. Vinny, I know I asked you to use the front door, but do you suppose you could include knocking or using the doorbell?

VINNY. Okay Ms. Scheller, for you I'll try, but it ain't somethin' I'm used to. I see you and the doc are, well... ya know...

JOAN. Yes, Vinny, we know. Is there something I can do for you?

VINNY. Jeez, Ms. Scheller, you and Doc here are good people. I just want ya to know it's nothin' personal if I have to rough up your boy a little if he shows up here.

JOAN. I don't suppose you could just go away and forget about this?

VINNY. You know I can't do that. This ain't chump change your boy owes. We gotta reputation to keep up.

JOAN. Well, do you suppose you could be here outside, without wandering in and out of our house?

VINNY. I can't do that. But just so's you know, even though I got a job to do, I'm watchin' out for you.

SANDY. What do you mean, "I'm watching out for you"?

JOAN. Yes Vinny, what do you mean?

VINNY. The feds are on to ya.

SANDY & JOAN. WHAT?

VINNY. I have it on good authority there's a federal agent around here who intends to bust you wide open, but ya don't have to worry 'cause we don't like the feds. I owe ya and I got your back.

JOAN. Oh dear. Sandy, what are we going to do?

VINNY. Leave it to me. What I want you guys to do is check the potting shed. Make sure it's locked and there are no chinks in the whitewash.

JOAN. Right, come on Sandy. *(**JOAN** takes the potting shed key from the back of the bar and exits the front door.)*

SANDY. I'm coming. *(Exits the front door.)*

> *(**VINNY** looks around and then moves behind the bar to pour himself a drink. **RACHAEL** enters from the French doors, but doesn't see **VINNY**, who quickly ducks behind the bar. **RACHAEL** crosses right for the script, picks it up, then looks toward the kitchen. She then looks around the room, back at the kitchen, and quickly moves upstage and exits into the kitchen, as **VINNY** tip-toes out from behind the bar and waits outside the kitchen door. **RACHAEL** re-enters with a brownie in her hand, but without the script.)*

VINNY. *(Stands directly in front of her, blocking her.)* Who are you?

RACHAEL. I'm Rachael, Mrs. Scheller's next door neighbor. Who are you?

VINNY. I'm Vinny the…um…the security guard. I'm Mrs. Scheller's security guard, and I know all about you.

RACHAEL. You do? Why?

VINNY. It's my buisness to know. Just where do ya think you're goin' with that brownie?

RACHAEL. I'm, well... I couldn't help myself, besides it's only one little brownie.

VINNY. If I didn't know better, I would have fallen for that, but I do. So, you ain't leaving here until you eat the evidence.

RACHAEL. You want me to eat it?

VINNY. Yep.

RACHAEL. Now?

VINNY. If ya know what's good for you.

RACHAEL. *(Looks at the brownie.)* Oh, I definitely know what's good for me. *(Pops the whole thing in her mouth.)*

VINNY. Okay, you can go now, but if ya know what's good for you, you'll stop trying to get at those brownies.

RACHAEL. They're really good. I had one yesterday and it made me feel quite expired.

VINNY. Well if ya don't stop trying to get them out of here, that can be arranged.

RACHAEL. What can? Oh, I forgot my script. *(She quickly enters the kitchen, followed by* VINNY, *who gets right up to the door as* RACHAEL *comes back out and flattens him with the door. The door swings closed, and* VINNY *slowly crumples to the floor as* RACHAEL, *unaware of* VINNY, *exits through the French doors.)*

(Enter OLIVIA *from down right.)*

OLIVIA. *(Sees* VINNY *on the floor and goes to help him up.)* Vincent, whatever are you doing sitting on the floor?

VINNY. I'm not sure.

OLIVIA. Are you feeling alright?

VINNY. I guess so.

OLIVIA. Then come along, stand up.

VINNY. *(Now standing.)* She plays it pretty cool, but she'll have to do better than that to keep me down.

OLIVIA. Whatever are you talking about? Did you hit your head?

VINNY. *(Crosses to behind the bar.)* Nah, I'm fine. I just need a drink. *(Takes the cap off of a bottle of beer.)*

OLIVIA. That sounds wonderful. *(Moves downstage and sits right on the couch.)* I'll have a martini with a twist, and an olive please.

VINNY. I ain't no bartender.

OLIVIA. I am not a bartender.

VINNY. You neither, then you're out a luck…how about a beer?

OLIVIA. No thank you Vincent. *(Pats the seat next to her.)* Please, come and sit down. I know you have to be tough and strong to be a security guard, but did anyone ever tell you how cute you are.

VINNY. *(Sits left on the couch.)* Well, Ms. St. Claire…

OLIVIA. Please, call me Olivia.

VINNY. Well Olivia, I ain't never been called cute before.

OLIVIA. I have never been called cute before.

VINNY. You ain't?

OLIVIA. You haven't.

VINNY. Well, I think you're a real good lookin' broad. *(Sets his drink on the table.)*

OLIVIA. *(Moves closer left toward* **VINNY.***)* Vincent, how very sweet of you. *(Holds his hand.)*

VINNY. Whoa there, what ya doin'?

OLIVIA. What do you mean, what am I doing?

VINNY. You was hold'n' my hand.

OLIVIA. You were holding my hand.

VINNY. No, you was hold'n' mine.

OLIVIA. Yes Vincent, I was. *(She takes his right hand in hers. There is an awkward pause. Then* **VINNY** *inches toward her and gives her a peck on the cheek. She pauses, looks at him, and then straddles him, with her back to the audience, and covers him with kisses as* **JOAN** *and* **SANDY** *re-enter from the front door.)* Oh, Vincent.

(JOAN *moves downstage toward the couch.* SANDY *puts the potting shed key back behind the bar, then follows her.*)

JOAN. Olivia, what are you doing on the couch with my security guard?

OLIVIA. *(Quickly stands, and we see* VINNY *'s face is covered with lipstick marks.)* I...ah...well, I was helping Vincent.

JOAN. Doing what?

VINNY. *(Stands.)* We weren't doin' nothin'.

OLIVIA. *(To* VINCENT.*)* We weren't doing anything.

VINNY. That's what I said, we weren't doin' nothin'.

OLIVIA. Actually Joan, I was following Doctor Gardener's advice.

VINNY. Ya were? Me too.

JOAN. *(To* SANDY.*)* Who do you think you are, Sigmund Freud?

SANDY. *(Smiles and pauses, and in a Freudian accent:)* What do you think?

OLIVIA. Vincent, there's a bathroom in the pool house, why don't you go clean up.

VINNY. Why'd I want to do that?

(OLIVIA *whispers in his ear,* VINNY *looks horrified, whips out a handkerchief, and rushes out the French doors.)*

JOAN. So Doctor Gardener, what's your secret?

SANDY. What do you mean?

JOAN. Getting everyone to follow your advice so quickly after just one session with you.

OLIVIA. He's quite inspiring to those of us willing to listen. Poor Joan.

CHRIS. *(Offstage.)* Mom?

(*Enter* CHRIS *from the front door. He is casually dressed in shorts, t-shirt, and loafers without socks.*)

CHRIS. Hey there. Aunt Olivia? What are you doing here?

JOAN. Chris? What are you doing here? *(She panics, runs to the French doors, and looks out.)*

OLIVIA. Hello Christopher. What a lovely surprise. I'm here for your mother's birthday. *(Looks over at **JOAN**, who is nervously looking out the French doors.)* Joan, are you feeling alright? *(There's no reply.)* Poor Joan, I can't imagine why she's acting so strangely. *(**JOAN**, clearly very agitated, moves right a step or two, then thinks better of it, returns to the French doors, and exits briefly.)*

SANDY. She has her reasons.

OLIVIA. I'm sorry, where are my manners? Christopher, have you met Doctor Gardener?

CHRIS. Nope.

SANDY. *(Shakes hands with **CHRIS**.)* Hello, nice to meet you. Your mother has told me a lot about you.

OLIVIA. He's your mom's psychiatrist, and from the way she's behaving I'm beginning to see why you're needed Doctor Gardener.

CHRIS. Psychiatrist?

JOAN. *(Rushes back in and gives **CHRIS** a hug.)* Oh Chris, it is good to see you, and in one piece. *(Looks back at the French doors.)* Did anyone see you come in? Why are you here?

CHRIS. Have you forgotten, it's your birthday.

JOAN. That's very nice of you to remember dear. *(Runs quickly toward the French doors to peek out.)*

OLIVIA. Yes Christopher, how very thoughtful. Joan, come away from those doors and talk to your son. *(**JOAN** looks at her, then out into the garden. Finally she crosses to **CHRIS**.)* Well Christopher, I can't wait to hear all about how you're doing, but I am sure you'd like some time alone with your mother first. Besides, I do need to freshen up a bit, I'm sure I'm looking simply wretched. I'll visit with you later. Ta ta. *(Exits down right.)*

CHRIS. I see Aunt Olivia hasn't changed much.

JOAN. No she hasn't. And apparently you haven't either.

CHRIS. What's that supposed to mean?

JOAN. Honey, I'm afraid you've got to go.

CHRIS. Why? I just got here.

JOAN. Sandy, you tell him.

SANDY. Well...uh... I'm not at liberty to say. Hippopotamus oath you know.

CHRIS. Mom? Does it have something to do with you needing a psychiatrist?

JOAN. Psychiatrist? I don't need a psychiatrist. Er...er... I mean... Chris, you might as well know, but please don't say a word as I haven't told your Aunt Olivia yet, Doctor Gardener and I are engaged. *(She grabs SANDY's hand and kisses him on the cheek.)*

SANDY. We are?

JOAN. Definitely.

CHRIS. Congratulations Mom. *(He gives her a kiss on the cheek.)* When did this happen?

SANDY. Very recently. *(JOAN gives him "a look.")* Look Chris why don't you come and sit down a moment. *(SANDY sits right on the couch and JOAN sits left on the couch. CHRIS sits in the chair.)* There is something else we need to tell you. The reason you can't stay here is that there's a mobster staking out the house. His name is Vinny and he calls himself "The Enforcer." He says you owe money and he's here to collect it from you.

JOAN. Chris, however did you get into this mess?

CHRIS. Sorry Mom, it just seemed to happen. I didn't mean for you to get involved.

SANDY. Well, we are, so I'm afraid you'll just have to leave. It's best for everyone.

JOAN. I'm sorry Chris. I want to help you, but it's just not safe for you to be here.

CHRIS. That's okay Mom, I'll leave.

SANDY. How did you get here?

CHRIS. I drove. My car is parked out front.

JOAN. Oh dear, he knows your car. He'll know you're here if he sees it. *(Crosses to the French doors to look out.)* The last time we saw Vinny he was going to the pool house. I just don't know how we're going to get you out of here without him seeing you.

SANDY. Maybe we can sneak him out the back kitchen door. Joan, quick, check that Vinny's not out there.

> *(JOAN exits to the kitchen. SANDY moves to the kitchen door and holds it partially open, waiting for JOAN's reply. CHRIS follows behind him. SANDY looks around and sees VINNY about to enter through the French doors. He quickly opens the door wide, with CHRIS behind it, and stands there looking nonchalant.)*

VINNY. *(Enters through the French doors, talking on his cell phone.)* You think ya saw him comin' in the house? Yeah, that's his car. You stay with the car, and I'll search the house. If he's here, I'll find him. *(Hangs up and puts the cell phone in his pocket.)* Ya wouldn't be hidin' someone in that closet would ya Doc? *(Strides over and opens the closet door.)* Uh, I guess not. Maybe the kitchen? *(VINNY exits into the kitchen as SANDY quickly gets CHRIS into the closet and closes the door, then continues holding the kitchen door open as VINNY moves back into the living room.)* Well, well Doc, what's hidin' behind door number three? Let's have a look.

SANDY. Why not. *(He releases the kitchen door.)*

VINNY. Gotcha ya little slimeball. *(Deflated.)* He ain't here either. So, where's he hidin' Doc?

JOAN. *(Enters from the kitchen.)* There's a... Oh Vinny, you're back. *(Looks around for CHRIS.)*

VINNY. Look Mrs. Scheller, we know he's here and he ain't goin' anywhere. My partner's watchin' his car, so are you gonna produce him, or am I gonna search the rest of the house?

SANDY. If you really feel it's necessary, by all means Vinny, search the house.

VINNY. Jeez Doc, ya know I got a job to do. *(Exits down right.)*

JOAN. *(Whispers.)* Where is he?

SANDY. *(Opens the closet door, and* **CHRIS** *steps out.)* Joan, we can't keep this up. He knows Chris is in the house.

CHRIS. Doctor Gardener's right Mom.

JOAN. I'm not turning my son over to the mob. We simply have to find a way to hide him until Vinny gives up searching for him.

SANDY. Have you been eating more brownies? That's not going to happen.

OLIVIA. *(Offstage.)* Vincent, I expect you to wait for an invitation to my room.

VINNY. *(Offstage.)* Jeez, sorry, didn't know you was in there.

JOAN. Oh dear, Sandy do something, he'll be back any second now.

SANDY. I'm not a magician.

JOAN. *(Looks toward the couch.)* I know, time for a session with Doctor Gardener.

SANDY. Now?

JOAN. *(Quickly sits with her feet up on the couch, head right, feet left.)* Chris, get over here. Now, lie down with your head here. *(She points to her stomach, and* **CHRIS** *lies down on his back. His feet protrude over the arm of the couch.)* Sandy, quick, cover us up. (**SANDY** *now places the afghan over them. It reaches from* **JOAN** *'s upper body to* **CHRIS** *'s mid-calf, giving the impression of one body [see Authors' Note].)* Sandy, quick his shoes. (**SANDY** *quickly whips off* **CHRIS** *'s shoes and returns to his chair, hiding the shoes behind him.)*

VINNY. *(Enters from down right, looks around, and moves toward the kitchen.)* I'll tell ya this, that boy of yours is a slippery one. *(He flings open the kitchen door and looks in.)* Ah-ha.

JOAN & SANDY. *(Look at each other, pause, smile, and simultaneously mimic* **VINNY**.*)* Ah-ha.

VINNY. *(Turns and quickly opens the closet door.)* Ah-ha.

JOAN & SANDY. *(Look at each other, pause, smile, and simultaneously mimic* **VINNY**.*)* Ah-ha.

VINNY. *(Closes the door.)* I don't understand it, my nose tells me he's real close by.

JOAN. What are you, a bloodhound?

VINNY. *(For the first time, he notices the strange figure of* **JOAN**. *There is a long pause as he looks at the couch from behind, then paces off the distance from her head to* **CHRIS**'s *feet. Eventually he scratches his head.)* Jeez, Mrs. Scheller, just how tall are you?

SANDY. *(Stands.)* Really Vinny, this is too much. We appreciate your help with our other little problem, but you cannot expect us to tolerate your continual intrusion into the privacy of our home. If you insist on this ridiculous search for Mrs. Scheller's son, kindly restrict your activities to the exterior of the house.

VINNY. That's it. Outside. He's in the pool house. Ciao. *(Exits, running out the French doors.)*

JOAN. *(Removes the afghan, and* **CHRIS** *sits up and moves left on the couch as* **JOAN** *sits right.)* He's not going to give up looking, is he.

SANDY. *(Hands* **CHRIS** *his shoes.)* It doesn't look that way. Chris, just how much money do you owe them?

CHRIS. Twenty thousand, give or take. *(Starts to put his shoes on.)* Maybe I should just turn myself in to him. What's the worst that can happen?

JOAN. I watched *The Godfather*, I know what happens, so that is definitely not an option. Wait a minute. *(Pauses.)* I've got another idea. *(Jumps up and quickly exits downstage right.)*

SANDY. Oh dear.

CHRIS. Oh dear?

SANDY. When Joan gets that look in her eye it only means one thing.

CHRIS. What's that?

SANDY. Trouble.

RACHAEL. *(Enters through the French doors and moves right.)* Hi there Doctor Gardener. *(Sees* **CHRIS***.)* Oh, am I interrupting a session?

SANDY. *(Stands.)* Not at all, let me introduce you to Joan's son. Chris, this is Rachael, your mom's new neighbor.

RACHAEL. Hi, nice to meet you.

CHRIS. *(Stands.)* Hello, *(Shakes* **RACHAEL***'s hand.)* the pleasure's all mine. Mom never mentioned having such a gorgeous neighbor.

RACHAEL. *(Giggles.)* Well, I only moved in recently, but thanks. Do you live here?

CHRIS. Nah, I'm just here for Mom's birthday.

SANDY. Is there something I can do for you?

RACHAEL. Well, I came to apologize to you, and to Joan's security guard.

CHRIS. Mom has a security guard?

SANDY. It's a long story.

CHRIS. *(Moves behind the bar.)* Would anyone care for a drink? *(Starts to pour himself a drink.)*

RACHAEL. No thanks. You see Doctor Gardener, I came back to get my script which I left in the kitchen, and the brownies were just sitting there, but before I could leave, he said *(Imitates* **VINNY***.)* I'd better eat the brownie if I knew what was good for me.

SANDY. Who said that?

RACHAEL. The security guard. So, of course I ate the brownie. *(To* **CHRIS***.)* Have you tried your mom's brownies? They're quite moorish.

SANDY. Moorish?

RACHAEL. You know, when you want more of them.

CHRIS. When did Mom take up baking?

SANDY. Er...er...quite recently.

RACHAEL. *(Starts to wander around the room.)* You know I use to work in this cute little bakery on the outskirts of town, that is until it caught fire and burned down. But it really wasn't my fault. I got to work early so I could make the cookies, and was just about to take them out of the oven when the phone rang. Part of my job was to take orders, so this guy was giving me this huge order, and kept changing his mind. My boss always said to put the customer first, so by the time I was finished, there were flames shooting out of the oven. They blamed me for not watching the cookies and I got fired. Go figure. But I still love to bake. *(Moves toward the kitchen door and peeks in.)*

> *(SANDY sees VINNY, who is about to come through the French doors. He motions for CHRIS to duck down.)*

VINNY. *(Enters and sees RACHAEL entering the kitchen. He runs toward the kitchen.)* Don't ya worry about a thing Doc, I got this under control. *(Exits through the kitchen door.)*

> *(CHRIS pops his head back up, and SANDY motions for CHRIS to go out the window. Just as VINNY reaches the kitchen door, RACHAEL re-enters from the kitchen, eating a brownie, and hitting VINNY with the door. VINNY slowly crumples to the floor.)*

RACHAEL. Oh dear, did I do that?

SANDY. *(Bends over VINNY.)* Quick Chris, you'd better get moving before he comes around.

VINNY. *(Opens his eyes.)* Too late. *(Points at CHRIS.)* You! I am goin' to personally fix your wagon.

> *(CHRIS dives out the window as VINNY gets to his feet and moves left to the window, followed by RACHAEL, who is right behind him. VINNY looks out the window, turns quickly, and bumps into RACHAEL. She grabs the vacuum cleaner to gain her balance and pushes it forward as VINNY runs into it. He trips, spins around, bumps his head on the wall, and slowly crumples to the floor again.)*

RACHAEL. Oh dear, I hope he doesn't have a conclusion.

SANDY. What?

RACHAEL. You know, a head trauma.

SANDY. I'm sure he'll be alright. *(Crosses to the French doors, followed by* **RACHAEL.***)* Chris, Chris are you out there?

CHRIS. Right here. *(Enters through the French doors and sees* **VINNY.***)* What happened to him?

SANDY. He met Armageddon.

RACHAEL. It really wasn't my fault, he just kept getting in my way. Why was he chasing you?

CHRIS. Well...er...er... Well, I kind of owe him some money.

RACHAEL. He's not very nice about it. I remember a time when...

SANDY. Rachael, thanks for stopping by. I'll let Joan know you were here.

CHRIS. I hope to see you again sometime.

RACHAEL. Me too, bye. *(Exits through the French doors.)*

SANDY. Okay, you hide in the kitchen and I'll get rid of him. *(***CHRIS** *exits to the kitchen, as* **SANDY** *shakes* **VINNY.***)*

VINNY. *(Sits up.)* Where'd they go?

SANDY. Who?

VINNY. *(Standing up.)* That walkin' disaster area and the slimeball, that's who.

SANDY. She went home and he went out the window.

VINNY. *(Takes out Bertha.)* Well if he knows what's good for him, he'll turn himself in to me, before my partner gets him. He's as mean as a snake. Sorry Doc, gotta job to do. *(Exits running through the French doors.)*

JOAN. *(Enters from downstage, with a dress on a hanger and a wig on a stand.)* Where's Chris? *(Moves upstage.)*

SANDY. *(Crosses to the kitchen door and holds it open.)* It's safe now – *(Looks at* **JOAN** *and the dress.)* I think.

CHRIS. Hey guys – *(Enters from the kitchen and moves left toward* **JOAN.***)* I'm really sorry about all of this.

SANDY. Not as sorry as I think you're going to be.

JOAN. I believe I've found the solution to our problem.

CHRIS. What is it?

JOAN. *(Holds the dress in front of* **CHRIS.***)* Perfect.

CHRIS. What?

JOAN. It's the perfect disguise.

CHRIS. Mom, I'm not wearing a dress.

JOAN. *(Pulling him by the hand toward downstage right.)* He'll never find you this way.

CHRIS. We'll never get away with this. What about the you know whats. *(Cupping his hands under imaginary breasts.)*

JOAN. Right. *(Looks around, sees the balloons, and grabs them.)*

SANDY. *(Moves toward* **JOAN.***)* Joan, just exactly what's going on now?

JOAN. Nothings going on. Come along Chris. *(She exits down right, followed by* **CHRIS.***)*

SANDY. Nothing's going on? Right. *(He crosses left behind the bar and pours himself a drink.)* This morning I was Sandy, Joan's lover, who agreed to be her gardener. Now, I'm no longer a gardener, I'm a psychiatrist. Olivia seems to be putting a move on a security guard who is really a mobster, our next door neighbor is clearly developing a taste for brownies, there's a federal agent snooping around, half the mob is outside wanting to break Chris's legs, and oh, I nearly forgot, I'm now engaged to a mad woman who says there's nothing going on.

OLIVIA. *(Enters from down right. She has changed into a fashionable day dress with matching shoes.)* Ah, Doctor Gardener, I'm so glad to catch you alone. I'd like to proceed with our last session. *(Moves toward the couch and sits left.)*

SANDY. *(Comes downstage.)* I really don't think...

OLIVIA. But I do not want to hear anymore about this group nonsense. *(Now lying on the couch with her head left and feet right.)* However, I want you to understand, we are definitely discussing the same topic.

SANDY. *(Sits in the chair.)* Olivia, I think you should know...

OLIVIA. Although this subject is slightly embarrassing for me to discuss, recent events have convinced me that I need to take charge of this area of my life. My question is how do I go about it?

SANDY. Um, well…what do you think?

OLIVIA. Well I did try, but now I don't know if I should wait or continue to jump right in?

SANDY. Well, if you're ready to start there's little point in waiting. I find that the earlier in the day you start the better. Preferably before breakfast.

OLIVIA. Before breakfast?

SANDY. Yes, I find if you have a good session before breakfast, you are often willing to go at it again in the afternoon, and on occasion, you might even be up for a third time later on.

OLIVIA. Three times a day?

SANDY. The more the better is my philosophy.

OLIVIA. I don't know if I can do it that often.

SANDY. Sure you can. Remember a good warm-up is important. Later on you can increase your stamina to improve your overall performance.

OLIVIA. Overall performance?

SANDY. Of course, it you do it more than once a day, you'll want to change your routine to keep it from becoming boring.

OLIVIA. Boring?

SANDY. You might even want to consider having more than one partner.

OLIVIA. More than one partner? Doctor Gardener, I though it was understood that I am not interested in this group thing you keep talking about.

SANDY. But I just thought…

OLIVIA. No buts Doctor. *(Sits up.)* I do however want to thank you for your time. You certainly have given me more to think about.

SANDY. Glad I could help.

OLIVIA. By the way, I was wondering, have you seen Vincent around?

SANDY. He, er...er...he said he had some business to take care of, but would be back later.

OLIVIA. Good, that's good. Do you know where Joan would happen to be?

SANDY. The last time I saw her, she was with Chris.

OLIVIA. *(Stands.)* All right then, if you'll excuse me, I think I'll just use this time to work on my autobiography. *(Exits down right.)*

SANDY. *(Looks around.)* I wonder if this is the calm before the storm?

VINNY. *(Enters from front door.)* We can't find him anywhere. *(Looks in the closet.)* I know he hasn't left here. *(Looks into the kitchen.)* He can't hide forever, and we aren't going to go until we get what we came for. *(Crosses to the French doors and looks out.)* Doc, just do me a favor and tell me where he is.

SANDY. I'm afraid I can't do that Vinny. I know better than to get in the way of a mama bear and her cub.

VINNY. You're a smart man Doc, but I just can't help but feel that he's right here under my nose.

JOAN. *(Enters from down right followed by* **CHRIS**, *who is now wearing a wig, dress, a pair of heels, and has balloons for breasts.)* Vinny, I don't believe you've met my daughter, Christina.

(Curtain.)

ACT II

(The action is continuous.)

VINNY. Hello there.

CHRIS. *(Gives a little finger wave.)* Hello.

VINNY. Wait a minute, wait a minute. I was never told you had a daughter. There ain't nothin' in our files about a daughter.

JOAN. Well – er – er – well there wouldn't be would there. You see I only just found out.

VINNY. *(Crosses right to get a closer look at CHRISTINA.)* How can you not know you had a daughter? That sounds awful suspicious to me.

SANDY. I'm sure Joan has a perfectly good explanation, don't you dear.

JOAN. Well of course I do. You see Vinny –

SANDY. Here comes another one!

JOAN. *(Gives SANDY a "look.")* Years ago, before I was married, I met Doctor Gardener while he was a student in med school. I was young and hopelessly in love. One thing led to another and well, I got pregnant. I didn't want to ruin Doctor Gardener's life so I left him and gave up our little girl for adoption. It was only recently that Christina tracked me down.

SANDY. I have a daughter?

CHRIS. *(Finger wave.)* Hello Daddy.

VINNY. *(Takes out a large red handkerchief and dabs his eyes.)* Ah Doc, this is a beautiful moment, ain't you gonna hug her?

SANDY. *(Moves down right.)* I suppose I can. *(He gives CHRIS a hug and one of CHRIS's balloons pop [see Authors' Note].)*

VINNY. *(Takes Bertha out, rushes back to the French doors, and looks out.)* What was that?

JOAN. I'm sure I have no idea.

VINNY. *(Now moving fast with Bertha in his hand.)* Nice meetin' ya Christina. **(CHRIS** *turns so that the side with the remaining balloon faces toward* **VINNY.)** Gotta check on my partner. *Ciao. (Exits through the front door.)*

JOAN. *(Moves up and sits on the couch, right end.)* Well that went pretty well don't you think?

CHRIS. Mom, this is a side of you I've never seen. *(Takes off the wig and holds it in his hand. He moves up to the couch and sits left end.)* When did you become such an accomplished liar?

JOAN. I never lie. I always tell some version of the truth.

SANDY. I now have a love child!

CHRIS. Hey Daddy, can you get me a replacement boob job.

SANDY. Oh right. Sorry about that. *(Gets another balloon from the bar back, hands it to* **CHRIS,** *and sits in the chair.)*

CHRIS. *(Stuffing the balloon into his dress.)* Listen you guys, I appreciate your help but we can't keep this up. Sooner or later he's going to figure it out.

RACHAEL. *(Enters from the French doors, now wearing a rain coat and carrying an open umbrella which she shakes, closes, and sets by the door.)* I just had to come back to tell you I've been thinking…

SANDY. I hope you didn't hurt yourself.

RACHAEL. *(Sees* **CHRIS** *and stops dead in her tracks.)* Oh! Oh my! You're wearing a dress.

CHRIS. Yes. *(There is a long, awkward pause.)*

SANDY. Joan, you're up!

JOAN. Ah, well, yes, you see, that's it!

SANDY. What's it?

JOAN. That's why he's here, to have a session with Doctor Gardener.

CHRIS. WHAT? Mom, I am not having a session with Doctor Gardener because I happen to be wearing a dress.

RACHAEL. Why not?

CHRIS. Because Doctor Gardener knows why I'm wearing this dress.

RACHAEL. He does?

CHRIS. Of course. Tell her Doctor Gardener.

JOAN. You're up, Sandy.

SANDY. I am?

JOAN. Yes, tell Rachael why Chris is wearing a dress.

SANDY. *(Grinning at* JOAN.*)* Sorry. Privileged information. Doctor patient relationship. (JOAN *glares at* SANDY.*)*

CHRIS. You're nuts, both of you. *(Stands, crosses left to* RACHAEL, *and takes her hands in his.)* Rachael, give me a couple of minutes to get changed and maybe we could go over to your place and get a cup of coffee or something, and I'll fill you in with what's going on.

JOAN. You can't do that. Vinny will see you. He's still out there somewhere, and if he finds you he's going to break your knees or something.

RACHAEL. Excuse me Mrs. Scheller, am I missing something? Why would your security guard want to do a thing like that?

SANDY. Yes Joan, why would your security guard want to do a thing like that?

JOAN. Well – um – er – it's like…

SANDY. Yes?

JOAN. Well – er – er…

SANDY. Come on Joan, Congress doesn't take this long.

JOAN. Right, well, it's like this.

SANDY. Here we go again.

CHRIS. Mom no. I want Rachael to know the truth about Vinny.

JOAN. Please, put the wig back on till we get things sorted out. He's still out there you know.

CHRIS. Oh alright.

> *(Puts the wig back on. Noises off from* **VINNY**.*)*

Come on Rachael, I need to explain some things to you. Let's just go down to the pool house for a few minutes. *(Grabs* **RACHAEL***'s hand as she hands him the umbrella. They exit quickly through the French doors.)*

> *(Enter* **VINNY** *from the front door.)*

VINNY. *(Comes down to the left end of the couch.)* That boy of yours is a slick one. He's not out front so he's gotta be here somewhere. Youse guys wouldn't be hidin' him, would ya?

SANDY. You've searched the entire house, exactly where would we hide him?

VINNY. That's a good question Doc. *(Pauses.)* And I know the answer.

JOAN. You do? Oh dear.

VINNY. You don't have to beat me with a meat mallet to figure this one out, he's in the potting shed. Ya want me to bust it open, or are ya goin' to give me the key?

JOAN. Better give him the key Sandy.

> *(***SANDY** *gets the key from the back of the bar and hands it to* **VINNY**.*)*

VINNY. Thanks Doc, just doin' my job. I'll be back after I check it out and give my partner a break. *(Exits through the French doors.)*

JOAN. See Sandy, everthing always works out.

SANDY. *(Sits in the chair.)* Isn't that what the Trojans said before they opened the horse?

JOAN. Well, it worked out for the Greeks didn't it?

SANDY. You are one of a kind, you know that?

JOAN. Well thank you, I love you too.

> *(Enter* **OLIVIA** *from down right.)*

OLIVIA. Hello you two, where is everyone?

JOAN. Oh, out and about. What can I do for you?

OLIVIA. *(Sits on the couch left.)* Well, I wouldn't mind one of your brownies if they're done.

JOAN. Really?

OLIVIA. Well a girl has to indulge sometime in her life.

SANDY. Well said! I'm sure Olivia will love your brownies.

OLIVIA. See Joan, it's just what the doctor ordered.

> (**JOAN** *exits to the kitchen.*)

SANDY. So how is your book coming along?

OLIVIA. Quite well actually. Thanks to you.

SANDY. *(Laughing.)* Why thanks to me?

OLIVIA. Although I do find some of your suggestions quite disturbing, you did get me thinking about when, where and who.

SANDY. I did?

OLIVIA. To be honest, I haven't exactly figured out the when and where, *(Giggles.)* but I'm pretty sure about the who.

JOAN. *(Enters from the kitchen with a brownie on a plate, which she hands to* **OLIVIA** *as she sits on the couch right.)* Here you go.

OLIVIA. *(Bites into the brownie.* **JOAN** *and* **SANDY** *both lean in slightly toward her.* **OLIVIA** *pauses, then looks at the brownie and takes another bite.* **JOAN** *and* **SANDY** *lean in even further.)* Delicious!

SANDY. I told you she would be fine.

OLIVIA. *(Finishing the brownie, she starts to giggle.)* Do you have any more?

JOAN. She's giggling, she never giggles. I knew this wasn't a good idea.

> (Enter **CHRIS** *through the French doors, still dressed as* **CHRISTINA** *and holding the umbrella, followed by* **RACHAEL**, *still in her rain coat. He folds the umbrella and sets it by the upstage French door.)*

OLIVIA. *(Giggling.)* Chris, is that you? Why are you wearing a dress?

CHRIS. Well... I...er...

OLIVIA. *(Giggling.)* Poor Joan.

JOAN. "Poor Joan" is bad enough, but a giggling "Poor Joan"?

CHRIS. Enough is enough. *(He takes the wig off and places it on the bar. He then tries to unzip the back of the dress, but can't. To* **RACHAEL.***)* Could you get this zipper.

RACHAEL. Sure. *(She starts to hum as she slowly undoes the zipper.)*

> (**CHRIS** *takes off the shoes and tosses them over his shoulder. He then steps out of the dress, revealing rolled-up pants, a white t-shirt, and a bra stuffed with balloons.* **RACHAEL** *picks up the dress and continues to hum while dancing and twirling the dress.)*

Take it off big boy, take it all off.

> (**CHRIS**, *getting into the spirit of things, starts to shimmy and hum while taking the balloons out of the bra one at a time and throwing them in the air.* **RACHAEL** *unfastens the bra, and* **CHRIS** *continues to slowly take off the bra. He twirls it around and throws it at* **OLIVIA**.)

OLIVIA. *(Catches the bra.)* Oh my. Poor Joan. Well if you can't beat them, join them. *(Giggling, she stands, moves center stage right, and starts twirling the bra over her head.)*

> *(She is joined by* **RACHAEL**, *who drops the dress in* **SANDY**'s *lap.)*

JOAN. *(Stands and moves upstage, picking up* **CHRIS**'s *shoes.)* Sandy, do something.

> *(At this point they are still humming.* **OLIVIA** *is standing just above the chair.* **RACHAEL** *is about three feet to her left. They have shimmied themselves down to a bending position, with each holding*

> *one end of the bra.* **CHRIS** *is downstage below*
> **RACHAEL**.)

VINNY. *(Enters through the front door and sees* **CHRIS**.) Gotcha you slimeball. *(He runs downstage toward* **CHRIS** *as* **OLIVIA** *and* **RACHAEL** *stand up, each still holding one end of the bra.* **VINNY** *runs into it across his chest, ricochets backward, and falls down.* **OLIVIA** *drops her end of the bra and bends down over* **VINNY**, *leaving* **RACHAEL** *standing alone holding the bra.)*

OLIVIA. Vincent, are you alright?

VINNY. *(Sitting up.)* Where'd he go?

JOAN. Chris, run!

> **(CHRIS** *starts to run out the French doors.)*

VINNY. *(Unsteadily gets up.)* Bad idea kid, very bad idea. *(Takes out Bertha and exits running after* **CHRIS** *through the French doors.)*

OLIVIA. *(Chases after* **VINNY**.) Vincent, where are you going? Why are you chasing my nephew. Vincent, I need to talk to you, wait up… *(Exits the French doors.)*

VINNY. *(Offstage.)* You're not getting away slimeball.

OLIVIA. *(Offstage.)* Vincent, do not use that name with my nephew.

VINNY. *(Offstage.)* There's no way out kid. Stop or I'll break your knee caps.

OLIVIA. *(Offstage.)* Vincent, I demand that you stop threatening him immediately.

JOAN. *(Moves downstage.)* Sandy, don't just sit there, do something.

SANDY. What do you suggest?

RACHAEL. Maybe we could…

CHRIS. *(Enters on the run through the front door, followed by* **VINNY**.) Mom, do something! *(Exits the French door followed by* **VINNY**.)*

OLIVIA. *(Enters the front door, panting heavily, and sits on the couch left.)* This is too much.

CHRIS. *(Offstage.)* Put the gun away and I'll stop.

VINNY. *(Offstage.)* Me and Bertha give the orders around here.

RACHAEL. Chris is in trouble. We have to do something

JOAN. We will. *(She drops the shoes in SANDY's lap, then moves upstage to the bar and grabs the wig.)* Rachael, your rain coat, take it off and bring it over here. *(She stands just below the right end of the bar.)*

> *(RACHAEL throws the bra to SANDY, then takes off her coat and stands four to five feet to stage right of JOAN, as CHRIS re-enters running through the front door. He stops between JOAN and RACHAEL who help him into the rain coat, which he quickly starts to button, while JOAN puts the wig on his head. He hurries down and sits in the chair that SANDY just vacated. SANDY quickly stuffs the dress, bra, and shoes behind the couch pillow, left side, and stands behind the chair. CHRIS crosses his legs nonchalantly as VINNY enters on the dead run and stops just beside the chair left side and stares at CHRISTINA. JOAN moves downstage and stands by the couch left, as RACHAEL moves toward the French doors and picks up the umbrella.)*

SANDY. *(Steps between the chair and VINNY.)* Can we help you Vinny?

VINNY. *(Shaking his head as he holds Bertha.)* I don't get it Doc. I coulda sworn I saw him come in here. This just ain't my day.

OLIVIA. It's, it isn't my day, Vincent.

VINNY. Yours neither eh?

RACHAEL. *(Now brandishing the umbrella in a sword-like movement toward VINNY.)* Take this you brute. *(She swings the umbrella and hits VINNY's hand, causing him to drop Bertha. RACHAEL immediately drops the umbrella and bends down and picks up the gun. VINNY makes a slight move toward her and she points the gun at him.)* Okay Vinny, make my day!

*(At this point everyone is on their feet, tentatively backing away from **RACHAEL**. She slowly sweeps the gun in a wide arc from upstage left to downstage right. As she does this, everybody ducks as they come into her sight-line. She then slowly sweeps the gun in reverse, and everybody ducks again.)*

SANDY. *(Crosses to **RACHAEL** and gently takes the gun from her.)* Perhaps it would be better if I had the gun. *(He hands the gun back to **VINNY**.)* Please put this away.

OLIVIA. Yes Vincent, put it away.

*(**VINNY** holsters the gun.)*

SANDY. Boy Vinny, you're not looking so good.

VINNY. Gee Doc, I don't feel good. I never had no problems catchin' slimeballs before. Maybe it's a sign I should be givin' this up. What do you think Doc?

SANDY. What do you think?

VINNY. I think I need some fresh air. *(Exits through the French doors.)*

CHRIS. Hey Rachael, thanks for your help. You were fantastic. *(Takes off the rain coat — with one sleeve turned inside-out — and the wig, and places them on the bar far right side.)*

SANDY. Joan, you must see by now that we can't keep this up.

CHRIS. Doctor Gardener's right Mom, we can't keep doing this.

SANDY. Listen, why don't I go and try to keep Vinny busy, while you try to figure out what to do. *(Exits through the French doors.)*

OLIVIA. *(Stands.)* All right you guys, I demand to know what's going on.

JOAN. Well, it's like this…

CHRIS. No Mom, everybody sit down. *(**JOAN** sits on the couch right side, **OLIVIA** on the couch left side, **RACHAEL** sits in the chair. **CHRIS** remains standing.)* Aunt Olivia, what you don't know is that Vinny is not Mom's security guard.

He's an enforcer from the mob, sent to make me pay some debts that I've run up.

OLIVIA. My Vincent, an enforcer? Poor Joan.

CHRIS. Actually it's not Mom's fault. I never intended for anyone to be involved in this mess.

RACHAEL. But, we are evolved.

JOAN. At least some of us are.

OLIVIA. Why don't you just pay him?

JOAN. We don't have the money.

OLIVIA. How much is it?

CHRIS. Give or take…about twenty thousand.

OLIVIA. Well, that's simple enough, I'll just write him a check.

CHRIS. I can't let you do that.

RACHAEL. Of course you can. I like you better when you're not wearing a dress.

CHRIS. Oh dear, this is getting complicated. Mom, Rachael, I need to be alone with Aunt Olivia.

JOAN. *(Stands and heads toward the kitchen.)* Fine, we'll be in the kitchen. Come along Rachael.

RACHAEL. *(Stands and follows JOAN.)* Are there any brownies left? *(They exit to the kitchen.)*

CHRIS. *(Moves to the kitchen door, listens for a second, then sits in the chair.)* Aunt Olivia, I want you to promise me that what I'm about to tell you remains between you and I. You must swear not to tell a soul.

OLIVIA. My lips are sealed. But I do have just one question. Why were you wearing a dress?

CHRIS. That was another of Mom's brilliant ideas to get me out of here safely. She wanted to fool Vinny into believing I was her daughter, Christina.

OLIVIA. Poor Joan.

CHRIS. She was just trying to help. You see, Mom doesn't know any of this and it's best that she doesn't. She'd only worry herself sick. I've been working for the FBI for nearly two years now. My so called gambling debts are part of an undercover operation to find out who the real mob bosses are in this part of the state.

OLIVIA. You work for the FBI?

CHRIS. *(Nods.)* You may not know this, but the FBI has been so successful in eliminating the mob bosses in the major cities, that they have moved into some of the smaller towns. My assignment is to find out who Vinny's boss is. The problem is that if you pay the money at this point in time without discovering who is behind this, I will have wasted about a year of my time.

OLIVIA. Oh Chris, this is exciting.

CHRIS. Aunt Olivia, this is not a movie, these are some really bad-ass guys.

OLIVIA. Why Vincent is just a big pussy cat. I can handle him. Now how can I help?

CHRIS. I don't want to get you involved.

OLIVIA. Nonsense, you're my nephew and I want to help.

CHRIS. Well, perhaps there is something you could do. Vinny is very smart and very careful. He never contacts his boss on a cell phone because he knows we would trace it in a heartbeat. If you really want to help, you could tell Vinny that you'll pay the money, but you must insist on talking directly to his boss before you do. If you can persuade him to use a cell phone, yours if possible, we'll probably be home free. Of course you'll get reimbursed later.

OLIVIA. How would I go about that?

CHRIS. Aunt Olivia, you can be pretty persuasive when you want to be. I'm sure you'll think of something. And I'll be right here to protect you if something goes wrong.

OLIVIA. Nothing will go wrong. This is going to be fun! *(She reaches behind the pillow, grabs the clothes, and hands them to* CHRIS.*)* If I were you, I'd find a new designer. *(She stands and moves downstage right.)* I'd better go and freshen up. *(Stops right before the archway.)* Vincent won't know what hit him.

CHRIS. *(Follows* OLIVIA.*)* I don't believe he will. Why don't I join you for a few minutes and I'll explain how cell phone tracking works. *(Gives her a kiss on the cheek.)* Thanks Aunt Olivia. *(They exit down right.)*

> *(Enter* VINNY *through the front door. He moves past the bar and suddenly stops. He slowly turns back and notices the rain coat and wig on the bar. He looks forward again, and then slowly walks backwards three steps and picks up the wig in one hand and the rain coat in the other and looks slowly at them. He sets them back down and slaps his forehead as if to say, "I've got it." He quickly turns and runs out the front door.)*

JOAN. *(Enters from the kitchen followed by* RACHAEL, *who is eating a brownie.)* I realize Chris isn't perfect, but he really is a very good son. If we get through this, I just hope he'll settle down. *(Sits on the couch right.)*

RACHAEL. Chris is just so sweet. I really hope things do work out with Vinny. Do you think he really intends to hurt him? *(Sits on the couch left.)*

JOAN. He's an enforcer, it's his job.

RACHAEL. Oh dear, you know that reminds me of the time when I got arrested.

JOAN. Whatever did you get arrested for?

RACHAEL. Well, it was a gorgeous day, so I decided to go to the beach. I was driving along I-95 when this kangaroo jumped out into the middle of the road. I swerved to miss it and hit a light pole.

JOAN. Don't you mean a deer or something?

RACHAEL. Oh no, it was definitely a kangaroo. Well, by the time the police arrived it had of course hopped away. When I told them what happened, they thought I was drunk or something and arrested me for obstructing justice by lying to them.

JOAN. You know dear, it's always best to tell the truth. That's my motto anyway.

RACHAEL. But I was. It turned out it had escaped from the zoo. There was a big article in the paper and everything. Of course they had to drop the charges. So you see, everything turned out fine in the end. I'm sure it will for Chris too. It's important to keep a positive altitude.

JOAN. *(Laughs.)* I'm sure it is. I just hope Doctor Gardener feels that way after today.

RACHAEL. Speaking of Doctor Gardener, may I ask you a question?

JOAN. I'd rather you didn't, but I suppose you're going to anyway.

RACHAEL. I don't mean to be nosey, but I have noticed Doctor Gardener keeps going into the potting shed and locking the door. Why does he do that?

JOAN. Right, er – um – well – um – you see… *(Pauses, then beckons to* RACHAEL *to lean forward.)* He has a deeply personal problem.

RACHAEL. Really? What is it?

JOAN. We don't ever talk about it.

CHRIS. *(Enters from down right.)* Well you two, everything alright in here? Nothing new to report?

JOAN. *(Stands, moves toward* CHRIS, *and kisses him on the cheek.)* Everything is just fine, for the moment anyway. If you'll excuse me, I think I'll go and see if I can find Sandy, er – I mean Doctor Gardener… *(Exits through the French doors.)*

RACHAEL. *(Stands.)* I guess I should be going. *(She moves upstage toward the bar and picks up the wig.)* You know, I've always wondered what I would look like as a **[insert wig color]**. *(Puts the wig on her head.)*

CHRIS. *(Follows her.)* You look adorable, but I like you better as a **[insert Rachael's natural hair color]**.

RACHAEL. *(Still wearing the wig, she picks up her rain coat and begins to put it on.)* I'd be happy to stay and help if you need me.

CHRIS. You've been amazing, but I think it's best if you go home now and I'll see you when this is all over. (**RACHAEL** *struggles to get her second arm in the sleeve because it is inside-out.*) Here, let me help you.

> (**CHRIS** *sees the inside-out sleeve and puts his own arm in it to pull it out.* **RACHAEL** *twists and* **CHRIS**'s *arm remains stuck in the sleeve. They twist, turn, and struggle, becoming more entangled in the rain coat.* **VINNY** *enters from the French doors.* **CHRIS** *and* **RACHAEL**, *in one desperate movement trying to untwist themselves, begin to fall behind the bar.* **RACHAEL**, *unseen by* **VINNY**, *falls first, but* **VINNY** *does see* **CHRIS** *as he falls.*)

> (**VINNY** *takes out Bertha and begins pacing up and down.*)

VINNY. I've got you this time youse slimeball and there's no way out. You might have thought you could outsmart Vinny, but I know what you're up to and you can't fool me any more. Come on out of there with your hands up, if you knows what's good for ya. (**VINNY** *Stops with his back toward downstage right at the back of the chair as* **RACHAEL** *slowly stands up, wearing the rain coat and wig, with her hands up and her back toward* **VINNY**.) Okay now, I want youse to take off your clothes.

OLIVIA. (*Enters from down right with a cell phone in her hand, which she puts on the coffee table, just as* **VINNY** *says his last sentence.*) Vincent, it's I want you to take off your clothes.

> (**VINNY** *suddenly turns around toward* **OLIVIA** *as* **RACHAEL** *indicates to* **CHRIS** *that he should go out the window.* **CHRIS** *dives head-first out the window.*)

VINNY. You do?

OLIVIA. Of course not, that would be inappropriate. However, I demand that you apologize to Christina for that outrageous remark.

VINNY. But *(Turns back toward* **RACHAEL.***)* that ain't Christina, and I'll prove it. Okay Christina…take off your clothes… NOW! *(***RACHAEL***, still facing upstage, slowly removes the rain coat, and puts it on the bar.)* Take off the dress girlie.

OLIVIA. Vincent, really, I must insist that you stop with all this utter nonsense.

VINNY. I'm sorry Ms. Olivia, but this is business. Now take it off. *(***RACHAEL** *slowly slips off her dress to reveal a slip.)* Okay, now the wig. *(***RACHAEL** *takes off the wig and sets it on the bar, as* **VINNY** *turns around toward* **OLIVIA.***)* I want youse to meet *(Turns back around.)* Chr… YOU! *(***RACHAEL** *does a finger wave as* **VINNY** *runs behind the bar.)* He's not here. I coulda sworn I saw him. Wait a minute, wait a minute, I know you, you're that agent.

OLIVIA. What agent? Vincent, what are you talking about?

VINNY. *(Moves downstage.)* She's an agent.

RACHAEL. *(Putting her dress back on.)* Well, I used to be. You see, I had this job interning for a travel agency. My boss let me help this wealthy couple who were celebrating their fiftieth anniversary and wanted to go on vacation to South America. All I had to do was reserve the flight and get their hotels for them. Anyway he went to Egypt, and she ended up in Thailand. We never did find their luggage. You know, they complained to the owner and he blamed me, so I never got to become a real agent. Go figure.

VINNY. Oh, you're good, that is quite the cover-up story, but you're not fooling me. I'm keeping my eye on you. I'll be back just as soon as I find that slippery slimeball. *(Exits out the front door.)*

OLIVIA. Why does my Vincent insist on keeping his eye on you?

RACHAEL. I really don't know. I only have eyes for Chris.

OLIVIA. I must say Rachael, if you are interested in my nephew I have some concerns. It seems like the most extraordinary things seem to happen to you. It's as if you're a living, breathing, one person disaster area. If you are planning on dating my nephew, I think you should speak with Doctor Gardener.

RACHAEL. I'm not sure that's a good idea.

OLIVIA. Why ever not?

RACHAEL. Well… *(Motions for* OLIVIA *to come closer, then looks around.)* Do you know he has a deeply personal problem.

OLIVIA. Really? What is it?

RACHAEL. We don't ever talk about it.

(Enter JOAN *and* SANDY *through the French doors.)*

OLIVIA. Ah, Joan and Doctor Gardener, just the people we need.

JOAN. Well, it's nice to be needed.

OLIVIA. To be exact, it's Rachael that needs Doctor Gardener.

RACHAEL. I do?

SANDY. She does?

OLIVIA. You do. We were just talking about all the strange things that keep happening to you, and I think Doctor Gardener can help you figure out why. Now, come along Joan, it's very odd, but I'm craving another brownie. *(Links her arm in* JOAN*'s and they exit to the kitchen.)*

RACHAEL. Maybe she's right. *(Moves to the couch.)* Okay, let's do it. *(Lies down on the couch head right, feet left.)*

SANDY. Why do I keep letting this happen to me, first Joan, then Olivia, now you.

RACHAEL. What?

SANDY. Nothing. *(Sits in the chair and pauses.)*

RACHAEL. Doctor Gardener?

SANDY. Oh, right, right. *(Pauses.)* So, what's your problem?

RACHAEL. Well, according to Ms. St. Claire, I'm a living, breathing, one person distemper area.

SANDY. What?

RACHAEL. Why do bad things keep happening to me?

SANDY. What do you think?

RACHAEL. I think it's better if I don't think.

SANDY. Do you think that's why these things keep happening to you?

RACHAEL. Because I think or I don't think?

SANDY. What do you think?

RACHAEL. About what?

SANDY. Let's start over. Why don't you tell me about one of these incidents.

RACHAEL. Oh, there's so many. One really good one was when I got fired because I typed the letter "R" when it should have been an "X," and the result was a catastrophe *(Pronounced cat-as-trophy.)*.

SANDY. I really don't follow.

RACHAEL. Well, I was working for this charitable organization and my job was to design and print up thousands of posters for a benefit, which was being held in a beautiful mansion on the beach. There was going to be a huge auction with the final bid to be for an exotic three day getaway to a secluded tropical island. But, when the posters came back, instead of describing it as exotic, the poster said erotic.

SANDY. Oh dear.

RACHAEL. You know they blamed me, and I got fired from volunteering. I mean, who gets fired from a volunteer position? Go figure. Oh, oh, oh, that reminds me of another one. My boyfriend had just got a job as a newspaper columnist. He was on a deadline, so I helped him out by typing up the article he was working on. He wanted to proofread it before it was sent to print, but I accidentally hit the send button.

SANDY. That doesn't seem so bad.

RACHAEL. Well, it turns out I had a slight typo, and instead of quoting the police chief as saying, "He thought the man should be incarcerated," I typed incinerated. The police chief was being called Hitler, my boyfriend lost his job, and I lost my boyfriend. All because of a simple mistake. Go figure.

SANDY. I'm beginning to see a common thread here. It sounds like you went through a bad *(Slight hesitation.)* spell. *(Chuckles.)* Sorry, couldn't help myself.

RACHAEL. So, what's wrong with me?

SANDY. There's nothing wrong with you, you're just one of those incredible people who are able to bounce back from disaster. That's a wonderful trait. *(Moves to sit next to her on the couch.)*

RACHAEL. Really? Do you really think so? Then I'm not just incontinent?

SANDY. *(Quickly stands up.)* Let's hope not. I would call you – er – resilient.

RACHAEL. *(Jumps up from the couch and kisses him on the cheek.)* Thank you Doctor Gardener. This has been so helpful. *(Calls out.)* Ms. St. Claire, Ms. Scheller, you can come out now. Doctor Gardener says I'm recipient and I'm cured.

(Enter JOAN from the kitchen, followed by OLIVIA.)

JOAN. It's been all of five minutes, how do you do that Doctor Gardener?

SANDY. *(Preens and grins at JOAN.)* Privileged information. You know, doctor-patient relationship.

OLIVIA. He really is remarkable. I wonder why you haven't been more successful with him. Poor Joan.

RACHAEL. Oh, I just can't thank you enough. I feel like a new woman. You know, I think I'll go look for Chris and invite him to come over for dinner tonight, after Vinny goes away of course. I'm not even worried that I'll burn down the kitchen. But first, I think I'll just have one more brownie for the road. *(Exits to the kitchen.)*

SANDY. She really is a unique individual isn't she.

JOAN. She does seem sweet, when the world isn't falling down around her.

CHRIS. *(Enters running through the front door.)* Hi guys. Vinny found me again, any suggestions?

> *(VINNY enters through the front door and sees CHRIS, who runs out the French doors, followed by VINNY.)*

JOAN. I've got an idea.

SANDY. Then we're all in trouble.

JOAN. *(Crosses to the bar, picks up the wig and rain coat, and hands the wig to OLIVIA.)* Olivia, quick, help me get Sandy into these.

SANDY. *(Getting into the rain coat.)* Joan, you're insane, this will never work.

OLIVIA. *(Places the wig on his head.)* Now what?

JOAN. Sandy, quick in the chair. *(SANDY sits in the chair, facing downstage.)* Olivia, the closet door.

> *(OLIVIA opens the closet door, holding it open. JOAN is now standing by the corner of the wall, just downstage of the plant, as RACHAEL enters from the kitchen and takes a step upstage.)*

> *(CHRIS enters from the front door on the dead run and comes down to JOAN's left. She takes his right hand in her left hand, and acting like a pivot, swings him across her body, transfers his right hand to her right hand, and all in one movement, swings him into the closet as he grabs RACHAEL's left hand and pulls her into the closet with him. OLIVIA closes the door and strikes a nonchalant pose as VINNY charges in through the front entrance [see Authors' Note]. He comes downstage two or three steps and suddenly stops level with JOAN. He stares at the back of SANDY's head and looks at JOAN, who smiles at him. He looks at SANDY again, then looks at OLIVIA, who smiles at him and finger waves.)*

VINNY. *(Again looking at SANDY, he starts to take out Bertha and takes a few steps forward.)* Oh no, not this time. I'm onto your little game. So Mr.

I-Think-I-Can-Outsmart-Vinny-The-Enforcer, if you know what's good for you, don't make a move.

JOAN. Vinny, please, put the gun away.

OLIVIA. Vincent, I will not tolerate any violence.

VINNY. *(Moves down level with the chair.* SANDY *is still facing right.)* Youse two need to stay out of this. Now tough guy, take off the wig. *(*SANDY *slowly removes the wig and turns toward* VINNY.*)* Doc? I don't believe it. *(He moves quickly down left and looks out into the garden.)* But why Doc? I thought we was friends. I even told youse all about Bertha, and I was thinking about parting ways with her and all, but now, I just don't know.

OLIVIA. Vincent, I demand to know exactly who Bertha is and what she means to you.

VINNY. I can't talk right now, I got a job to do. *(He walks slowly back to the center of the room.)* Don't anyone go nowhere till I find that son of yours. *(Exits to the front entrance.)*

JOAN. *(Opens the closet door, revealing* CHRIS *and* RACHAEL *kissing.)* Alright you two, you can come out now. *(They don't move, so she pulls them out of the closet while they are still lip-locked.)* Really, Chris, this isn't a good time for this. *(*CHRIS *waves her away as she reaches into the closet and pulls out three identical rain ponchos.)* Olivia, we're going to need a little time. Can you keep Vinny out of here for just a few minutes?

OLIVIA. Is the Pope Catholic? *(Exits front entrance.)*

SANDY. *(Stands and takes off the rain coat, laying it and the wig over the back of the chair.)* Why do I have this feeling we're all in trouble?

JOAN. *(She tries to pull* CHRIS, *but they continue to kiss with both of them moving.)* Sandy, do something about this.

SANDY. Right. *(Moves upstage toward* JOAN *and kisses her.)*

JOAN. Oh my! That wasn't quite what I meant, but I'm not complaining. *(Hands* SANDY *a rain poncho.)* Here quick, put this on.

SANDY. Why?

JOAN. We need a decoy. *(SANDY puts on the poncho.)* Chris, you need to listen. Here, put this on. *(JOAN picks up the wig from the back of the chair.)* I think Olivia has another one of these. You two, follow me. Rachael, I think you'd better go home. *(During this line, she separates CHRIS and RACHAEL and hands CHRIS one of the ponchos, while continuing to hold the other.)*

CHRIS. Mom's right. *(Kisses RACHAEL quickly.)* I'll call you later when the coast is clear.

> *(JOAN, SANDY, and CHRIS exit downstage right. RACHAEL grabs her rain coat and exits through the French doors as OLIVIA enters through the front door, followed by VINNY. They move downstage.)*

VINNY. How many times do I gotta tell you, I don't want to talk about Bertha.

OLIVIA. How many times do I have to tell you, I do not want to talk about Bertha.

VINNY. If that's so, why are we still talking about her? *(Sits on the couch right side.)*

OLIVIA. Vincent, please stop being obstreperous. *(Sits on the couch left side.)*

VINNY. How can I when I don't even knows what youse is saying? You should speak normal like me. Maybe you should talk to the doc about it. He's real good.

OLIVIA. Speaking of Doctor Gardener, have you heard?

VINNY. What about him?

OLIVIA. *(Motions for him to sit closer to her on the couch, then looks around.)* He has a deeply personal problem.

VINNY. Oh no, not Doc.

OLIVIA. Oh yes, Doc.

VINNY. Really? What is it?

OLIVIA. We don't ever talk about it.

VINNY. Why that's real decent of you. You knows what Ms. Olivia? You may be high falutin and all that, but I think inside you, you can be a real nice lady sometimes.

OLIVIA. Why thank you Vincent, and underneath all that macho facade, I think you're just *très debonair*.

VINNY. Whoa now, there you go again, not speakin' normal and calling me names. That's just not right Ms. Olivia.

(*In the downstage right entrance we see* JOAN *with* SANDY *and* CHRIS, *who are both wearing the rain ponchos and wigs. The hoods are up, so you can see a bit of blonde wig, but you cannot see their faces, leaving the audience to wonder who it is. They are visible only to* OLIVIA. JOAN *motions to* OLIVIA *to distract* VINNY.)

OLIVIA. (*Sidles up to him.*) Really Vincent, I was simply saying you have a sensitive side, which I find very attractive and irresistible. (*She pulls him down into her and kisses him.*)

(SANDY *quickly enters the room and moves toward the kitchen. As he goes past the couch he is seen by* VINNY.)

VINNY. (*Jumps up.*) Wait a minute, who was that? (SANDY *exits through the kitchen door, followed by* VINNY. JOAN, *watched by* OLIVIA *from the couch, takes a few steps onstage with* CHRIS *and indicates that he should go through the French doors.*)

CHRIS. (*Gives her a quick kiss on the cheek.*) You're unbelievable Mom. (*As* CHRIS *exits the French doors,* JOAN *exits down right, and* VINNY *re-enters through the kitchen door.*)

OLIVIA. (*Stands.*) Vincent, what are you doing back here?

VINNY. (*Crosses and sits on the right bar stool and unholsters Bertha.*) Well now little lady, my partner's out front so I reckon that slimeball ain't goin' anywheres far. I figures he'll be coming through that front door any second now, and I'll be waitin' for him.

OLIVIA. That's, he will not be going anywhere far.

VINNY. Ain't that what I said? Jeeze, why do you keep repeatin' what I say? Do youse need one of those hearing aid things?

OLIVIA. Vincent, I will not tolerate being spoken to in that manner. Now apologize.

VINNY. Sorry, I didn't mean to be rude to youse.

OLIVIA. I didn't mean to be rude to you.

VINNY. You didn't, gee, thanks. *(CHRIS enters running through the front entrance and runs right past VINNY, who points his gun at CHRIS.)* Come on in slimeball, come on in. Make yourself at home. *(CHRIS stops dead in his tracks.)* Now, youse just go sit in that chair there. *(CHRIS moves toward the chair, followed slowly by VINNY.)* I've gotcha now. *(CHRIS sits and VINNY takes a step toward him, his back to the French doors. He is about to remove CHRIS's hood, as SANDY enters through the French doors and begins to slowly move toward the bar.)*

OLIVIA. Vincent, I think you should look behind you.

VINNY. *(Stops.)* That's the oldest trick in the book. I'm not letting this slimeball out of my sight. *(SANDY, now behind the bar, coughs, causing VINNY to turn and see him. SANDY then ducks down behind the bar.)* Wait a minute, wait a minute. What's this? There's two of youse? *(Looks at CHRIS, then back at the bar as he furtively moves upstage toward the bar.)* Alright you, if youse don't want to be mincemeat, come on out of there.

> *(SANDY slowly stands up with his back to VINNY and his hands in the air, as CHRIS stands up and starts to take a few steps toward the French doors. VINNY swings back toward him, as SANDY starts to move from behind the bar, causing VINNY to swing back. JOAN enters from down right. She is wearing an identical rain poncho and wig. She takes a few steps forward then stops as VINNY swings back toward CHRIS and then sees her. He slowly walks with his back downstage, toward the French doors, pointing Bertha at each of them in turn.)*

This ain't possible, now I'm seein' things. I think this might be a sign for me to quit. Ms. Olivia, where's the doc, I need the doc. *(He gets level with the French doors,* as **RACHAEL** *arrives on the dead run and hits* **VINNY** *from behind. He goes down, with* **RACHAEL** *on top of him.*)

OLIVIA. (*Rushes down to* **VINNY.** **RACHAEL,** *apparently unhurt, stands as* **OLIVIA** *kneels by* **VINNY** *'s head.*) Vincent, are you alright?. Oh dear he's unconscious.

RACHAEL. Oh dear, I've done it again! Just when I thought I was cured. (**VINNY** *moans.*)

OLIVIA. He's coming round. Quick, Chris, get everyone, out of here. This is my opportunity to...you know.

CHRIS. Right, good thinking. Mom, Doctor Gardener, you've got to go, now.

JOAN. Chris I –

CHRIS. Please Mom, no questions, just do what I'm asking.

SANDY. Come along Joan. (*Pulls* **JOAN** *by the hand, and they exit down right.*)

CHRIS. Come on Rachael. (*Grabs* **RACHAEL** *'s hand, and they exit through the French doors.*)

OLIVIA. Poor Vincent, come and sit down sweetie pie. (*Helps him over to the couch.* **VINNY** *sits right and* **OLIVIA** *sits left.*)

VINNY. What happened?

OLIVIA. Rachael happened.

VINNY. Again?

OLIVIA. Again.

VINNY. You called me sweetie pie.

OLIVIA. Yes Vincent I did.

VINNY. I ain't never been called sweetie pie before.

OLIVIA. Vincent, it's I have – never mind. There's something very important I would like to discuss with you.

VINNY. Do you think I'm gettin' too old for my line of work?

OLIVIA. No Vincent I do not, but a new line of work is exactly what I'd like to talk to you about. However, we first have to solve the problem of Christopher's debts. I would like you to contact your superior immediately on your cell phone and find out the exact amount. Then I will write you a check. When all that's taken care of, I wish to offer you employment as my personal security guard.

VINNY. That's against the rules.

OLIVIA. What is?

VINNY. Using my cell phone.

OLIVIA. Very well then use mine. *(Picks up her phone from the coffee table and hands it to* **VINNY***.)*

VINNY. Oh, okay, I guess that'll be alright. *(Dials the phone.)*

OLIVIA. I wish to talk to your boss personally.

VINNY. Okay, but he's not my boss, he's a Capo.
(Into the phone.) Hey Mike, Vinny here. Looks like I'm about to get the money from the Scheller kid. The dame with the cash wants to talk to you. *(Hands her the phone.)*

OLIVIA. Hello Mister Capo.

VINNY. He's not Mister Capo, he's a Capo.

OLIVIA. Hello Mister A.Capo. *(Listens for a moment.)* Whatever! Just give me the amount Chris owes. *(Pauses.)* Very well, I will write Vincent a check. *(Pauses.)* What do you mean "you don't take no checks"? *(***VINNY*** reacts.)* *(Pauses.)* I see, then Vincent will simply have to accompany me to the bank. *(Pauses.)* Alright I understand, small bills. But, I want you to understand that this will be Vincent's last job for you, as he will be leaving your employ and starting his new career as my personal security guard. *(***VINNY*** reacts.)* Please watch your language, and his name is no longer Vinny the Enforcer, it is simply Vincent. *(Pauses.)* His salary? Not that it is any of your business, but Vincent will be well compensated while in my employ. *(Pauses, then laughs.)* Benefits? *(She leans over and kisses* **VINNY** *on the lips.)* I can assure you that you can not possibly match the benefits that Vincent will be receiving. *(Pauses.)* Very well, here he is. *(She hands the phone to* **VINNY***.)*

VINNY. Yeah, okay Mike. I'll have the cash later today. *(Pauses.)* Yeah, It's all true. Youse got that right. She is one bossy – (**OLIVIA** *gives him a "look."*) – I mean classy dame. *Ciao. (He clicks off the phone and hands it back to* **OLIVIA.***)*

OLIVIA. Well Vincent, I know you're a man of few words, but do you wish to say anything?

VINNY. Nope. *(Grabs* **OLIVIA** *and kisses her.)*

OLIVIA. With kisses like that, you don't need words.

VINNY. Okay, now let's go get that money.

OLIVIA. *(Stands.)* Just give me a moment to grab my purse and spruce up a bit. *(Moves down right.)*

VINNY. Don't be too long…sweetie pie.

OLIVIA. *(Giggles.) Ciao* Vincent. *(Blows him a kiss as* **JOAN**, *followed by* **SANDY**, *enters from down right.) Ciao* Joan, *ciao* Doctor Gardener. *(Giggles and exits down right, downstage of* **JOAN** *and* **SANDY.***)*

JOAN. *(Looking right.)* She's giggling again and I know it can't be the brownies. Vinny, you're still here? I don't think I can take much more. I need a drink. *(Moves up behind the bar and prepares a drink.)*

SANDY. *(Moves upstage to* **VINNY** *and claps him on the shoulder.)* Well Vinny, I see you survived another Rachael attack. How are you doing?

VINNY. Well Doc, despite all the attacks, being fooled by Christina, and then having three of youse guys trying to be decoys I don't think it could be much better.

SANDY. I'm delighted to hear that Vinny… So, you'll be going now?

VINNY. Soon Doc, soon. Ya know, there is just one little thing I'd like to discuss with ya before I go, but I'm not sure I should be talkin' to ya now.

SANDY. That didn't stop you before.

VINNY. That's exactly it, Doc. That was before.

SANDY. Before what?

VINNY. Before we all knew you had a deeply personal problem.

> (**JOAN** *coughs up her drink.*)

SANDY. I do? (*Looks across at* **JOAN** *who turns away, trying to be nonchalant.*)

VINNY. Oh yes.

SANDY. (*Looking directly at* **JOAN.**) May I ask what it is?

VINNY. (*Moves left and motions for* **SANDY** *to sit on the couch. He looks back at* **JOAN** *and leans in.*) It's okay Doc, I know, we don't never talk about it.

OLIVIA. (*Enters from down right, now carrying a purse and wearing different shoes.*) Come along Vincent, no dilly dallying, let's get to the bank. (*Moves upstage toward* **JOAN,** *followed by* **VINNY.**)

JOAN. Bank, did I hear you say bank?

OLIVIA. Oh, didn't I tell you, I'm paying off Chris's loan. Sorry you weren't in the loop. Poor Joan.

VINNY. See Ms. Scheller, now you don't have ta worry about my breakin' your boy's legs. That's one great sister-in-law youse got there.

OLIVIA. (*Copying his accent.*) Aw Vinny, youse really a great guy.

VINNY. I think that's, (*Copying her accent.*) Vincent you really are a great guy, (*Pauses.*) and thank you.

OLIVIA. (*Giggles.*) As Bogey would say, "I think this is the beginning of a beautiful friendship."

VINNY. "Here's looking at you kid." (*Gives* **OLIVIA** *a kiss on the cheek.* **OLIVIA** *hooks her arm through his and they exit through the front door.*)

JOAN. (*Still behind the bar.*) My, I don't think I've ever seen Olivia look so happy. This calls for a celebration, can I get you a drink?

SANDY. Thank you, a cold beer would be nice.

JOAN. Coming right up. It has been quite a day, hasn't it.

SANDY. Yes it has. You know sweetie, I was thinking, after today you could never be known as the ultimate liar.

JOAN. I'm glad to hear you say that, but why?

SANDY. You're over qualified. *(They both laugh.)* However, there is one little thing about today that I'd like to discuss with you.

JOAN. I can't imagine what that would be. Everything's turned out so well thanks to all my interventions. Olivia appears to be in love, Chris will stay in one piece, Rachael didn't burn the house down, and you can go back to being Sandy, the man I love and adore. Let's just enjoy the peace and quiet.

RACHAEL. *(Enters running through the French doors.)* Oh Doctor Gardener, there you are. *(She crosses right to the chair.)* Something terrible has happened!

SANDY. *(To JOAN.)* You had to go and jinx it. *(Stands, crosses left, and takes RACHAEL's hands in his.)* Whoa now, slow down, what is it?

JOAN. *(Moves to RACHAEL's right.)* It can't be all that bad.

RACHAEL. *(During the following speech she never stands still, moving from JOAN and SANDY, who remain standing just above the chair, to the French doors to look outside, and back left again and again.)* Oh it is, it is. You see when Chris and I got to my house, we heard the toilet in the bathroom running so Chris, being the great guy that he is, offered to take a look at it. He's just so sweet. Did you know he was so handy?

JOAN. What happened?

RACHAEL. It really wasn't my fault.

JOAN. *(Looks at SANDY.)* Oh – oh.

SANDY. So what's the problem?

RACHAEL. Well, Chris was bending over, looking into the bowl, and when I opened the door it hit him from behind and he went head first into the toilet.

SANDY. And?

RACHAEL. *(Almost in tears now.)* We couldn't get him out.

JOAN. And I was worried about Vinny breaking his legs?

SANDY. Okay, let's go.

RACHAEL. Oh, thank you. *(She turns to move toward the French doors just as* **CHRIS** *enters. His head and shoulders are soaking wet. He has a toilet seat wedged under his left arm and the right side of his neck. The lid is flopping on its hinges above and behind his head, and he has to keep one arm up to control it. He moves to center stage as she moves toward* **CHRIS**.*)* Oh Chris, are you alright?

JOAN. Well, he is looking a little flushed.

SANDY. *(Now walking around* **CHRIS**.*)* Amazing, I don't think I've ever seen anything quite like this.

JOAN. *(Walking around* **CHRIS**.*)* Oh my!

RACHAEL. *(Walking around* **CHRIS**.*)* I'm so glad you got your head out of the toilet.

SANDY. How in heaven's name did you manage to get it over your shoulder?

JOAN. You know, this reminds me of the time when you were just a little boy and we were on vacation somewhere. You had a fascination with...

CHRIS. MOM! It may not have occurred to you, but I am in a most uncomfortable, painful, not to mention embarrassing situation. It wasn't bad enough that I have spent half my day running around the garden, wearing a dress, trying to stop a mad man from breaking my knees. No, now for the first time in my life, I have had the wonderful experience of fighting my way out of a toilet. So, if you don't mind, I would prefer not to spend the rest of my life with a toilet seat stuck on my head.

SANDY. Quite right, here, let's get him into the chair. *(They all get him onto the chair.* **SANDY** *stands behind the chair and tries to lift the toilet seat. He just lifts* **CHRIS** *up with the seat.)*

CHRIS. OW! OW! OW!

RACHAEL. Please be careful.

SANDY. If it went on, it has to come off. I know, Joan can you sit on him please. Rachael can you put some weight on his shoulders?

CHRIS. If it's all the same to you, I'd rather it was Rachael on my lap.

SANDY. Right.

> *(With* **RACHAEL** *sitting on* **CHRIS***'s lap, and* **JOAN** *holding his shoulders down,* **SANDY** *wraps his arms around the toilet seat and twists it. There is a loud yell from* **CHRIS***, but this time it comes off.* **RACHAEL** *immediately kisses him as* **JOAN** *and* **SANDY** *take a step back to observe.)*

JOAN. They're at it again!

SANDY. Last time it took forever to separate them.

JOAN. Come on let's get them out of here. *(They get* **RACHAEL** *and* **CHRIS** *standing, and shuffle them, lip-locked, out of the French doors, then close the doors. She moves toward the couch.)* So, Doctor Gardener, how about a little session? *(She lies down with her head right and feet left.)*

SANDY. *(Follows* **JOAN** *right.)* You do remember, I'm not really a doctor.

JOAN. Of course I know that, but I really would like a session with the famous Doctor Gardener. I want to know why everyone thought you were so great.

SANDY. I'm afraid that won't be possible.

JOAN. And why not?

SANDY. Because...I have a deeply personal problem. *(***JOAN** *attempts to throw a cushion at him, but he reaches forward and grabs it before it leaves her hands, and falls on top of her.)*

OLIVIA. *(Offstage.)* Hellooo.

> *(***SANDY** *leaps up and is in the exact same position as he was when* **OLIVIA** *entered at the beginning of the play. There is a pause.)*

JOAN. Wait a minute. Isn't this where it all started this morning?

> *(Curtain.)*

FURNITURE AND PROPERTY LIST

ONSTAGE

Bar back
ON IT: Glasses, wine bottles, filled decanter.

A hook attached to the bar back
ON IT: Potting shed key attached to a large marijuana leaf key ring.

Bar: Under the bar should be a shelf
ON IT: Three beer bottles, bottle opener, pad, and pencil

Large potted plant
Two bar stools
A sofa
ON IT: Two couch pillows and an afghan

A low back chair
End table
Coffee table

ACT I OFFSTAGE

A tray
ON IT: Two coffee mugs, plate of brownies, and newspaper (**JOAN**)

Single rose (SANDY)
Vacuum cleaner in the closet (JOAN)
Gift basket
IN IT: Wine and blown up balloons (**OLIVIA**)

Suitcase (VINNY)
Wig on stand (OLIVIA)
Plate (RACHAEL)
Script (RACHAEL)
Christina's dress on a hanger, wig on a stand (JOAN)

ACT II OFFSTAGE

Golf-type umbrella (RACHAEL)
Plate
ON IT: Brownie (**JOAN**)

Three rain ponchos in the closet (JOAN)
Purse, shoes (OLIVIA)
Toilet seat (CHRIS)

PERSONAL

Magnum .45 gun (VINNY)

Wad of $100 bills (**VINNY**)
Handkerchief (**VINNY**)
Cell phone (**VINNY**)
Large red handkerchief (**VINNY**)
Cell phone (**OLIVIA**)

COSTUMES

Joan
Casual skirt or pants
Colorful blouse
Flat shoes
Wig

Vinny
Double breasted pin-strip suit
  (*Dark*)
Button-down shirt (*Yellow*)
Tie (*Red*)
Socks (*White*)
Fedora hat (*Black*)
Shoulder holster

Olivia
Designer skirt
Designer blouse
Accessories, handbag, and shoes
  to match
Sunglasses (*Large*)
Designer dress
Accessories and shoes (*Match dress*)
Hat

Sandy
Khaki pants, with belt
Button-down collared shirt
Socks
Shoes (*Loafer-style*)
Wig

Rachael
Simple dress

Camisole slip
Tennis shoes
Oversized rain coat

Chris
Shorts
T-Shirt.
Shoes (*Casual slip-ons*)

Dress (*See Joan's prop "dress"*)
Wig (*See Joan's prop "wig"*)
High-heel shoes
Bra
Inside: balloons

AUTHORS' NOTES

Page 20. The wigs should all be the same color and not the same color as Rachael's hair. If possible they should be long and curly so as to partially hide the faces of the other characters who wear them later.

Page 23. MALAPROPISMS. There is a definite technique for making sure the audience understands. The actor should always give a split-second pause before using the malapropism, in order to emphasize the word. If this is not done, the audience is liable to hear the correct word and not the malapropism.

Page 39. The total distance from the top of Joan's head to Chris's feet should be about seven feet. Any more would be beyond belief, any less would be too real, and therefore not funny.

Page 47. The safest and surest way to get this right, is for Chris to have a large pin concealed in his left hand, and, as Sandy hugs him, Chris pops the left balloon himself through the dress and bra.

Page 65. The elapsed time from Chris's entrance to the closing of the closet door and Vinny's entrance should be no more than three seconds. In the authors' opinion it is only funny if it is fast and slick. So – practice, practice, practice!

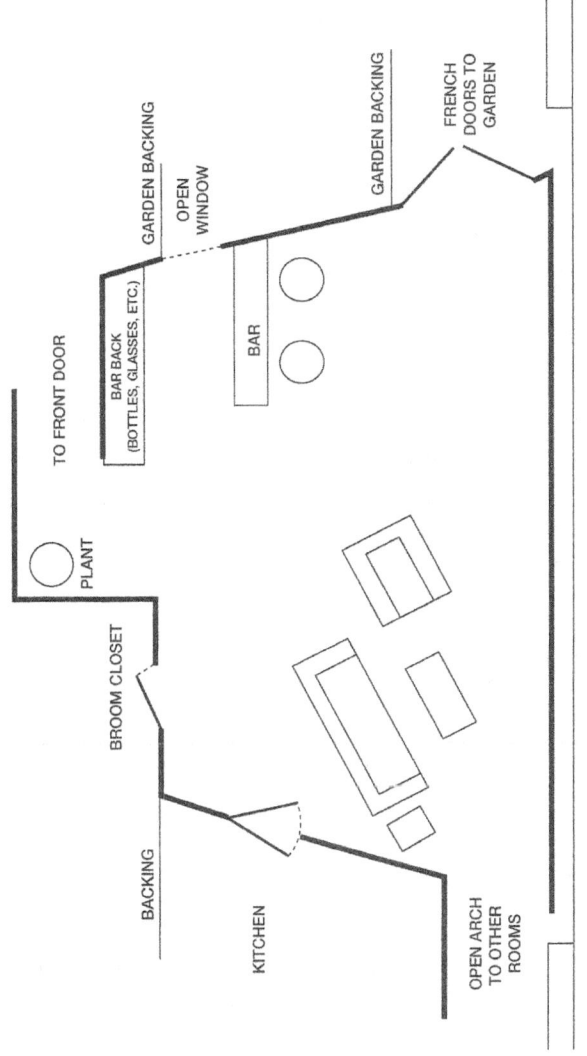

LOVE, LIES & THE DOCTOR'S DILEMMA

www.ingramcontent.com/pod-product-compliance
Lightning Source LLC
Chambersburg PA
CBHW071930130726
47909CB00014B/2854